PRAISE FOR

STUBBORN ARCHIVIST

Longlisted for the Desmond Elliott Prize

"I read *Stubborn Archivist* in a ravenous gulp. It's stunning: so articulate about what it means to live between two languages and countries, tenderly unravelling the knots of unbelonging."

— Olivia Laing, author of *The Lonely City* and *Crudo*

"*Stubborn Archivist* is an intimate and wonderfully resourceful exploration of origins. In its quest to uncover what a person is made of it digs deeply into the living body, as well as tracing back through its tangled roots. Visceral and elegant, circumspect and vivid, Yara Rodrigues Fowler has a distinctly unhampered way of telling a story; I liked *Stubborn Archivist* very, very much."

— Claire-Louise Bennett, author of *Pond*

"Intimate, rebellious, and meditative, Yara Rodrigues Fowler's exquisite deconstruction of a transnational life already in fragments will leave you spinning. *Stubborn Archivist* is wholly original and heralds the arrival of a remarkable new talent."

— Patricia Engel, author of *The Veins of the Ocean* and others

"Refreshingly experimental."

— *Independent*, "30 of the Best New Debut Novels to Read in 2019"

"Yara Rodrigues Fowler's debut is unlike any other book you've read. A blend of prose and poetry, it's a collection of short pieces that gradually cohere into a larger narrative . . . Holding the disparate elements together is a strong sense of identity and voice . . . Flitting nimbly through generations, between Brazil and South London, between dating and dictatorship, this is a novel that is personal and political—and its unusual form is integral to its power."

— *Observer,* "Meet the Hottest-tipped Debut Novelists of 2019"

"This novel beautifully explores the notion of home, belonging, and trauma for people who, like this Brazilian-English writer, find themselves growing up between languages and cultures and identities . . . A unique book you'll be able to read in one immersive sitting."

— *Elle,* "Ones to Watch: The New Writers We're Excited to Read in 2019"

"In this artful debut, snatches of dialogue and prose-poetry illuminate the experience of growing up with a mixed identity . . . Rodrigues Fowler [executes] it so well, so warmly, with such a lived sense of how nothing is one thing or another, but probably both and neither . . . Tender, sharp, generous, she holds all these things lightly, up to the light."

— *Guardian*

"Intimate and nonconforming."

— *Reading Women Writers Worldwide*

"This is undoubtedly the novel's strength: its ability to show something momentous—about cultural identity, sexual violence, racial prejudice—without seeming to say anything at all."

— *Times Literary Supplement*

"Yara Rodrigues Fowler has written something extraordinary, playing with structure to create an insightful, lyrical, and visceral novel."

— *Emerald Street*

"This is quite the debut. A book I feel I haven't read a hundred times before, and one which I suspect will stand up very well to a second reading."

— Fiona Melrose, Women's Prize long-listed author of *Midwinter*

"A timely exploration of what it means to understand past and present and the delicate balance of embracing two cultures simultaneously . . . Original and thought-provoking, this is a book that's well worth your time."

— *Stylist*

"*Stubborn Archivist* is a little like finding someone's notebook on a long train journey and reading it cover to cover by the time you reach your destination . . . It has the effect of being real."

— *The Skinny*

"Every page oozes with caustic wit, despair, and self-awareness, creating a lyrical debut that pushes the novel form like no other in recent years. A talent to watch."

— Nikesh Shukla, coeditor of *The Good Immigrant*

"My goodness. Yara Rodrigues Fowler has conjured a work of rare power, startlingly original form, and devastating beauty. This novel is a triumph."

— Musa Okwonga, author of *A Cultured Left Foot*

"A mixture of poetry, prose, and a smattering of Portuguese make this debut about growing up in a Brazilian-English household unlike so much else that we're told is a 'strong female voice' today. Equally assured discussing Sainsbury's, bad dates, or the intimacies of the second-generation immigrant's experience, Rodrigues Fowler's has a tone instantly recognisable to anyone who has lived in the UK, yet entirely individual. Her story of straddling two cultures as a young woman torn between them is charming, pithy, and moving."

— *Grazia*, "5 Female Authors to Read Before Everyone Else Does"

"What a treat. So lyrical, playful, and brave. I wish it had existed when I was younger, growing up between London and Brazil; it would have made me feel less alone."

— Luiza Sauma, author of *Flesh and Bone and Water*, on Twitter

"Compelling . . . Should delight anyone looking for a thoughtful, witty successor to Sally Rooney." — *Observer*

"An #OwnVoices triumph . . . A daring debut novel, when the narrative is a mix of stunning prose and poetry . . . We need more novels like this, novels that tell stories that haven't been told before. What is interesting about *Stubborn Archivist* is that it feels completely new, even though these stories have been told by word-of-mouth through generations of immigrant women. We need more novels that make people like me feel deeply seen as an immigrant, a Brazilian woman, and a daughter."

— Nicole Froio, *BookRiot*, "*Stubborn Archivist* Is Proof #OwnVoices Is Necessary"

"A visceral experiment in form and language . . . A novel with a sense of urgency . . . It is a novel overflowing with violence and depression and silence, but there is love, too, and skin sticky with golden honey . . . Yara Rodrigues Fowler's novel is an eloquent work of messiness, of ugliness."

—*Litro*

STUBBORN ARCHIVIST

Yara Rodrigues Fowler

A Mariner Original
MARINER BOOKS
HOUGHTON MIFFLIN HARCOURT
BOSTON NEW YORK
2019

First U.S. edition

hmhbooks.com

Library of Congress Cataloging-in-Publication Data
Names: Rodrigues Fowler, Yara, 1992– author.
Title: Stubborn archivist / Yara Rodrigues Fowler.
Description: Boston : Mariner Books, 2019.
Identifiers: LCCN 2018042566 (print) | LCCN 2018045915 (ebook) |
ISBN 9780358007067 (ebook) | ISBN 9780358006084 (paperback)
Subjects: | BISAC: FICTION / Literary. | FICTION / Contemporary Women. |
FICTION / Coming of Age.
Classification: LCC PR6118.O346 (ebook) | LCC PR6118.O346 S88 2019 (print) |
DDC 823/.92 — dc23
LC record available at https://lccn.loc.gov/2018042566

Book design by Chloe Foster

Printed in the United States of America
DOC 10 9 8 7 6 5 4 3 2 1

FOR MYSELF

Only a house as quiet as snow, a space for myself to go,
clean as paper before the poem.

– *The House on Mango Street,* Sandra Cisneros

PART I

The Big House

THE BIG HOUSE appeared from behind conker trees on a quiet street by the common.

It's late Victorian

Yes

These houses were built after the construction of the railway as they turned the farmland into the suburbs

Yes

They had come just the two of them, for one of the first times since the baby was born they were out together.

Richard opened the iron gate and stepped into the front garden. It was regrowing untidy with the spring.

He turned to his wife. We'll get rid of this gravel. I could plant a ceanothus here by the path.

Isadora looked at him. Which is that?

It has those tiny flowers that fall like grey blue dust onto the floor. Richard spread his arms — Over time it can grow into a large bush.

She nodded. It is very nice that one.

Richard stood inside the carved brickwork arch at the front of the house. He looked at the front door. He looked at Isadora.

She touched the morose little bird depicted in the off-brown stained glass of the door.

She looked at Richard.

We can get rid of this, no?

He paused.

It's depressing. I want bright yellow birds or soft orange squares or something.

He looked at the bird and then he looked at her.

She laughed at him — I'm serious Richard.

Inside, he ran his hand along the ribbed wall of the corridor, taking slow strides towards the back of the house.

Isadora stood behind him in the corridor. She regretted its closed door presence. Unlike her husband, she felt no secret thrill at its twee Victorian geometries — the cracked diamond tile floor, the textured wallpaper, the high up faraway light fixtures.

To their left there was a large bay window living room facing the street, and behind that a dining room facing the garden. Richard gestured to the second door — We could turn this into a TV room, or a playroom or a library.

But — she called her husband's name — but Richard, I don't see the point of such a big house.

He paused.

I like the little flat. We are just three after all. We don't need a big house like this.

He turned to face her.

I like the little flat. She approached him and put her hand on his arm — What's wrong with the little flat?

He frowned at her, and then he smiled. But what happens when your mum comes to stay, and your father? And don't you want Ana Paula to have her own room and not sleep on the sofa and be woken up when we go to work?

Isadora was quiet.

And eventually the baby will want her own space.

Isadora frowned.

It's only down the road. It's not a big change.

She put two arms around him. I know this. You are right. I just like the flat.

And then her husband said — Isadora this is a good house. Look.

They walked down the corridor to the dark kitchen that needed new cabinets. On the back wall there was a door and a set of concrete steps.

Richard opened the door.

Look at this garden.

Isadora looked at it.

Hot sunlight crossed its long and low sunk rectangle through the alley gaps between the other houses. It was full of knee height nettles and other grass green plants she didn't know the names of. At the back of the garden, by the fence, there was a row of lime trees.

Isadora was quiet.

Then she said — We could have a dog, Richard.

Her husband frowned.

Just a small dog, Richard. Woof woofwoof.

They were quiet.

Richard said — Where I grew up we had a huge garden. This is small but it's good for London.

Isadora nodded. At her parents' house Isadora had not had this sort of garden either.

Isadora chewed Richard's house words in her cheeks —

skirting board
mantel piece
banister

hearth
trellis
chimney
coving
terracotta
wallpaper paste

When she had thought of Europe, Isadora had always imagined herself walking into an open plan room with glass for walls.

That night in the flat, while the baby was asleep, Isadora whispered —

Richard did I ever tell you about my mother's yellow house?

Yes.

Oh. Isadora yawned.

Richard yawned.

My dad said he will put a pool there, for the baby.

That is very kind of him.

We could go at Christmas.

Christmas at the beach!

Yes.

I would certainly enjoy that —

The baby made a noise.

Of course, they bought it. Even in 1992 with the derelict house next door and the late night activity on the common it was all their savings and a mortgage it would take them twenty years to pay off, but they bought it. As Richard had said, this was a good house.

Both of them had been brought up to buy a house. Go to medical school, and then buy a house like we bought this house, their parents had told them.

And in the months after they had moved in, when the trees were full of leaves and tiny flowers were falling like blue dust onto the floor, Isadora took a photograph of her husband standing in front of the house, holding the baby. She sent it to her parents.

Both of them had been brought up to buy a house. Each of them was two generations away from someone who had built their own house in the earth and three generations away from some faceless predecessor who had never owned or built any house at all. (Isadora's mother had a little yellow house by the sea.)

But it was the late Victorians who had built this house. Although Richard sanded the floors and Isadora put up the bookshelves. And, that summer, as the baby who called to them in two languages learnt to walk, Richard planted a white and yellow rose bush in the garden, which was small admittedly but big for London.

And, slowly, Isadora unbuilt the house.

With each trip back she brought something new, covering small pieces of kitchen wall and staircase and armchair surface with twisty red blue orange blue colours. At first she brought small things — a ceramic bowl, a palm-sized wooden toucan, a little statue of a woman in a red dress dancing — and then big. Oversized checked baggage, does anyone have a spare suitcase big. Beaded yellow netting to hang from the picture rail, a huge abstract painting of a forest to go above the sofa, a green string hammock for the trees at the end of the garden.

And in the kitchen there was always orange yellow fruit in the fruit bowl and a pressure cooker on the stove. Isadora went to the market on the high street to buy dendê and shrimps and cassava and when the season was right ripe Kesar mangos that tasted as wet and soft as mangos from home. And after work she would try to cook the dishes that she had eaten as a child, and she would underdo them or over-salt them and lose her patience but when they sat down to eat Richard would say — Very nice! Very nice indeed.

This was the house that they would rush leave every late December, packing and locking and unzipping rezipping.

This was the house that they would quiet arrive to every January. Cold, staid and dusty, in need of arriving rewarming.

This was the big house that her baby would grow up in, that her baby would learn to walk in, in all its heated sofa space and down the concrete steps into the garden.

Years later, when they had the money again, Isadora insisted they got big glass doors at the back of the house — No, not like a conservatory, like a glass wall onto the garden.

This was her house unbuilding, her slow house mending.

Because after all, as Richard had said, this was a good house. This was the big house that meant that Isadora would never be poor, and that her baby would never ever be poor and would always be safe.

Stubborn Archivist

The first time we met

Hey — I recognise you

Yes

What's your name?

He repeated the syl-la-bles.

Yeah that's nice, where's it from?

It's from Brazil.

Jeeeez. He bent over and whistled. I love Brazilian girls though!

Ha, okay.

My name's Leo — he held out a hand formally, his hair flopped over his forehead — it's French, it means lion.

Oh right.

She paused.

Yeah there's a similar word in Portuguese.

He looked at her hard.

You speak Portuguese?

She looked back

Something I don't talk about and I regret

I can talk in Portuguese in bed
Okay yes do it
Okay

Kissing

At first there was standing up kissing
hands on face and jaw and waist kissing
And then there was up in the air legs around his hips
open mouth close mouth open mouth tongue kissing

And then lying down on the grass kissing
lying down on the sofa his whole body over her
everywhere over her
(murmuring between kissing)

this is how
this is how
this is how we'll do it kissing

Haircutting

One day he said, his hand on her neck —

Would you ever grow your hair?

I grow it all the time.

No. Seriously, you know past your chin let it get all long and flowing?

Yeah I don't think so.

All messy and all over your back!

I don't want messy hair. You've seen pictures — it wasn't as flattering.

I thought it looked nice.

No.

Especially when it was all in a bun and coming out

No, I like this. I look older like this.

Yeah, but you know you could have that sexy Eva Longoria, Penélope Cruz hair, falling all over the place

Yeah. But I like this. I look different, you know, Anna Wintour, Victoria Beckham —

Who's Anna Wintour?

Um you know the real life Meryl Streep from *Devil Wears Prada*.

Why do you want to look like her?!

I dunno.

I thought you liked my hair

I do.

Going out

For the two of them the nighttime was the best time. Anything can happen and everything is exciting when you're a sixteenyearold-pretendingtobeatwentyoneyearold in London at night.

These nights began always sat cross-legged on the floor, in her bedroom or in Jade's bedroom — whoever's parents were out. They played music through little speakers and spread all their make up and earrings and eyeliners and high heels on the carpet.

They planned, put their make up on carefully. Baby wipes ready, prepared if necessary to start it all over again. Beginning, clandestine, knowing, consultative, meticulously to wreak new adult faces hands and bodies.

This black dress?
No too young looking
What about the red one?
Looks like you're trying too hard
But —
I know but
What about these black jeans and the lacy thing?

Yes Mum I'm staying at Jade's tonight, I'll text you when I get there. Of course I'll be safe. Yes I'll say hi to her mum from you. Yes you can have a hug. Big hug big kiss

Dark lipstick

Red lipstick
Liquid eyeliner
a long swish soar in the night coat that had been Jade's mum's

They would go to the liquor store the corner, where they would talk too loudly about doing their tax returns, and then they would clickclack clack rush down the empty escalator and neck wine from the bottle on the Northern Line while playing drinking games, and nervously they read over the text from Jade's cousin's friend about how they didn't need ID but if anyone did ask –

And they would trip lipstick emerge into the glass streetlight dark where they never felt cold. Jade always knew the way through the big streets and the back streets to the doors that led down downstairs

And in the dark Soho night they would say –
I'm a fourth year studying zoology at Edinburgh
My name is Esmeralda
My name is Ana Paula
I'm a visiting student from Rio
And could my friend Esmeralda also have a cigarette?
Yeah actually you have a bit of an accent
My name is Minerva McGonagall

Not going out

Sometimes they never made it out, or ended up at a party down one of the quiet residential streets in Furzedown where all the houses had the same Victorian front room dining kitchen terraced set up and they ended up in a house with Elena and the boys in their year from school who sat at the back of someone's garden with their hoods up in the rain or in a shed smoking a too loosely rolled spliff and drinking cans of cider, and then there was that time that girl in the year below had had a party and they'd thrown her dad's vinyls around her muddy garden like frisbees.

One time when Jade's mum was away the two of them had stayed in and hadn't invited anyone else over except Elena and they drank the dusty fancy-looking whisky at the back of the cupboard in Jade's living room (refilling the green glass bottle with water and putting it back in the cupboard after) and they had drunk it on its own at first and then with orange squash. My mum has it with water, Elena had said, and they had shaken their heads in disbelief.

That night they laughed and then they cried and argued and cried again and Jade vomited into the wardrobe.

Leaving the house one night

Hey how you doing
Fine, thank you
Where you going darling
Out
You don't look like you're from here.

What?

Like, you don't look like you're from here
What do you mean?
Dressed so smart, you know
Well I live here I am from round here

Coming home

Men talked to her a lot. Especially on the night buses back south.

I have a boyfriend, sorry.

Nah you're just saying that

No really I do, his name is Leo.

Is it now

He's tall and handsome and he's going to be a doctor

Aw come on you didn't need to tell me that, I believe you you know.

Never have I ever

Never have I ever kissed a boy
Never have I ever kissed two boys in one night
Never have I ever kissed a grown up man

Never have I ever kissed a girl
Never have I ever had sex
Never have I ever tried to have sex

Never have I ever been drunk in front of my mum

Going *out* out

And in the dark Soho night there would be dancing

drunk tipsy where's my oyster card dancing
night bus first tube sunrise dancing
high heel red dress lipstick dancing

loud loud laughing Lydia Bennet laughing dancing

Honeymoon

They lay in his big bed. In his flat, which was just his to pay bills for and clean and decorate and walk around in because although she was still at school, he had left school now, was a serious adult student studying in the same hospital as her parents and what mother wouldn't approve of that.

They lay in his big bed, both naked and in that effusing enthusiastic, revelatory mood. The grey walls were dark grey in the twilight.

Propped on an elbow –

Well did you ever see me around school?

Yeah I had noticed you

Really?

Yeah! You know you're loud. Hard to miss. You held a door open for me once I think

Which one?

Um the one near the reception

I can't believe you remember!

You don't?

No!

Well I guess I was younger than you

What did you think of me, what did you notice?

Um

Did you think I was fit?

I don't know

Propped on an elbow

And what about me?

You

Yes.

Well I'd seen you around, but—you know—you were a bit young for me.

Not anymore

No.

But when we first met?

I was still with Stephanie then

I remember

But remember when I asked you what your name was

Yes

I did know it already

Oh yeah?

Yeah I'd heard of you, half-Brazilian

How did you know that?

Just did. I had a thing for Brazilian girls

Yeah?

Used to love Brazilian porn

Oh my god!

He turned his head and closed his eyes, and then looked at her.

Is that bad he said, touching her

Happy Birthday

At her eighteenth birthday party, in front of all those people, her parents and her friends from school, he had held her very close

There had been lots of music and some real champagne and beers that her parents had bought and fairy lights all down the concrete steps into the garden out of the house.

He had held her very close –

In a sort of a slow dance
She was drunk and he was drunk and everywhere the lights were low and the music was slow.
She couldn't really dance, not really

He whispered in her ear
    Step step step

She could not remember

His laugh
His breath
His elbows
His bottom teeth
The look of him asleep

Her laugh in his house
The smell of his breath on her breath

And what about his quietest laugh
The paper skin below his elbows

How had he held her name in his wet and whispering mouth

I never see you anymore

Jade, JadeJadeJade just come round to the flat –

Leo can go to the shop, we can get something to eat
And then?
I don't know

I don't know.

Even if she tried she could not remember

Any meal that they had eaten together

his breath
or his bottom teeth

A jumper she had bought him which he'd worn with nothing underneath warm from the bath in winter

his elbows

his bottom lip
his elbows

(one time, she dreamt he had a broken arm)

Approximately —
how many nights she had fallen asleep with her nose against the underside of his chin?

What he said he had wanted –

To see her in her pyjamas
Those little shorts
To wake her up, her cheeks swollen from sleep

again
and again
and again again

He was only a little bit older – that honestly wasn't the problem she was very mature for her age, everyone said so, she had read all the Jane Austen books at least twice and just like her mum (and just like her tia) she could sit exams with her eyes closed, or her eyes wide open as well as her mouth, laughing

He was only a little bit older. With his newly grown up body that grew from the ground all stretch white skin, his legs large from football, his broad shoulders his thin fingers, his chest that was still sprouting hair, his collar bones his neck, his long white narrow white finger bones that fanned like lizard gills covering his face

But what about the good times?

There were good times.

(yes)

There were good times

2014

THE IBS GOT her in the morning. She was stuck on the toilet like she often was before work. She brushed her teeth sitting down. It was probably the caffeine, or the dairy. Maybe it wasn't even IBS. She'd heard a radio programme about bowel cancer the other day, but you had to have blood in your shit for that and she didn't have blood in her shit. Just water.

She stood up. Her parents had already left the house for work. She touched her belly over her blouse and felt its bubbling. She put on the blazer with the wide sleeves. She went down the stairs and put her shoes on to leave. The thing about dressing like this and having a face like this is that no one thinks you are the source of the gas on the tube.

Twenty-five minutes later, at the end of the West End street she walked through big glass doors and swiped her swipe card. Standing in the lift she would remember to feel grateful.

It was unusual to get a good job like this straight out of uni.

In the lift, she thought to herself — It is unusual, and I am very lucky.

Or, as her dad had insisted — But they are very lucky to have a young kid like you with your languages and your cultural know-how.

Sometimes she got gas in work meetings but so far it had been manageable.

She was a researcher for a new documentary about plastic surgery in Brazil. All the women in Rio were getting plastic surgery — in their butts and tits and noses and out of their stomachs. Her job was to find potential participants, to make sure they were the best ones and then get them to agree to appear on the show. They had given her her own thick plastic landline telephone with the curly wire that called Rio directly and a desk and an email address and a chair she could swing her feet under. We want ordinary women, the producer Fiona had said in the kick-off meeting. Women who have been saving for months and months, who are going into debt, you know?

Mmhm.

Her first task had been to use online directories to make a spreadsheet of all the beauty salons and surgeons and pageants and modelling agencies in Rio. Today she would begin calling the salons. She scrolled up and down the spreadsheet. She dialled the number of the first salon. Typed it in, typed it wrong, typed it in again. Beep

She waited. She heard a click and an older woman's olá bom dia voice on the other end. She took a breath —

Bom dia. Eu sou uma jornalista inglesa —

She looked around the office. Her feet under the chair. She could have been saying anything.

Bom dia. Eu sou uma jornalista inglesa —

The woman on the other end was the owner of the beauty salon. She did not hang up the phone.

So, that afternoon, having spent twenty years spelling out her foreign name to English people, she spelt out her foreign name over the phone to the woman in the beauty salon.

She said — I'm sorry it's quite long and it's got an English bit in it. Sorry —

Her email address was a nightmare. She braced herself before announcing its interminable phonemes, steeling herself for the relief of the @.

And she was always careful to reassure the participants that they would come off well.

That morning she had come in late (there's no point you being in before people are up in Brazil, the producer had said) and so that evening she left the office late when it was fully dark.

On these days, when she came home late after calling Brazil on the plastic landline telephone, she always got a seat on the tube. She played tetris. Sometimes she played candy crush. She had one audiobook on her phone which she listened to on repeat.

Elephant and
Kennington
This station is Oval (no it's not)
Clapham
Clapham
Clapham

Clapham

At home at the house, she found the bowl of spaghetti with tomatoes and cheese covered in clingfilm that her parents had left out on the stove for her. She unwrapped it and touched it with her finger. She held it under her nose. It smelt wholesome with the taste of bay leaves from the garden.

She put the bowl of spaghetti in the microwave. Her parents had not heard her arrive. They were still watching the news on the sofa. She leant on the kitchen counter with her eyes closed. She heard the ping. She went up the stairs quietly.

In her room, she took off her skirt and her tights. She ate the warmed up dinner under the covers in her childhood bed. She opened her laptop and turned on a TV series that she had seen before. She closed the curtains. When she finished eating, she left the bowl on her bedside table and opened tetris on a second window on her computer. When she couldn't focus her eyes anymore she turned the volume low so that the TV voices became speaking sounds with no words or phrases.

And in the night images of the pink and yellow shapes slotted and reslotted in her mind and when she went to sleep they covered the faces of all the people in her dreams.

So things were kicking off, really.

She worked in TV. She was on twitter. She had a thing and that thing was Brazil.

She had been invited to write for a big political blogger's site. This had happened on a watery day in February that wasn't as cold as it should have been because of global warming. Nathan who was also a researcher had introduced them over drinks after work. I have a friend you should meet, Nathan had said.

They had stood under the wet awning between hanging flower baskets outside one of the pubs near the office. She was quiet and knew she should be speaking.

Nathan said – This is Alex.

She looked at Alex.

Hi. Alex shook her hand. Hi.

Hi Alex.

What's your name?

She told him, and he repeated the syl-la-bles.

He looked at her.

What a lovely name. Where is it from?

Brazil.

And are you – ?

Yes.

But you sound so –

Well yes I was born here

Right

In London, in South London actually.

Alex was a bit older than her with Harry Potter glasses.

My dad's English.

So you're half and half?

Yes.

But you were brought up –

Bilingual.

Bilingual? So you speak it just like you speak – he waved his hands – I mean *gosh* that is just –

Well no, not exactly the same.

Right.

But we go back a lot. Usually for Christmas. I was there this Christmas just now actually.

He looked over at her through his glasses.

She took another drink of her drink.

Nathan looked at her then back at Alex.

Alex said – Oh-kay. Interesting.

The next day Alex emailed her while she was at work asking her to write about Brazil from the Brazilian perspective. But like, for English readers? You know, there's a lot of buzz about Brazil this year. We want you to tackle the difficult subjects, the gritty stuff, you know?

But

When they published her first piece she got the shits. And when they published her second piece she got the shits. She lay on the cold floor of the bathroom. Her mum asked through the door — Are you okay baby? Loo-confined and sweating. She couldn't open her laptop or look at her phone. She took a shower. Sat in her dressing gown.

Lay in her childhood bed.

Back when she'd met the Brazil-end producer of the plastic surgery programme the woman had said – Olha só your eyes are so striking. Light against your dark hair. My husband is English, my children are half and half like you.

In her bed she lay down in the darkness listening to the tetris shapes.

Once a uni friend had asked her why she said she went back at Christmas –

Why is it back? Her friend had said.

Late one weekday evening when it was dark her mother knocked on her bedroom door, holding a bowl of yoghurt and rice.

Can I come in?

Yes.

Her mum lay on the bed next to her, over the duvet. There was a quiet. She knew that her mum was looking at her.

She felt the duvet tension shift under her mother's body.

Her mum held out the bowl.

She took it.

She felt embarrassed.

She felt grateful.

What had happened was — she had left, but now she had come back. She had left saying brave and angry hopeful things like —

I just want to leave London
Tooting Tooting Tooting
I'm finally grown up
Look how big the world is

Got her own loan and a laptop and a budget and a mini fridge and whatever else.

So she had left, but now was back.

Not taller or bigger breasted like she had imagined she would be at that age, but able to smell the smell of the house, the roasting vegetable humidity it had in the evenings, and the dusty dryness of it when no one was home.

At least once or twice a week in her adult daytime life she would run into someone from the year below at school or someone's mum or someone's brother's ex-girlfriend on their way to return a pair of shoes (because these are a six, and technically I'm a six-and-a-half, but Topshop actually doesn't do half sizes so) or see the new Batman movie or a job interview or get their iphone fixed or whatever or whatever. Ideally she would see them first and walk in the opposite direction, or look down and squish away from them in the full up tube carriage. Second best was when they would talk about themselves (yeah I'm a manager now at the new pub on the high street, I don't know if you know it, it's a bit wanky but at least people know how to behave themselves there do you know what I mean)

But sometimes it happened the worst way, a girl from two years above at school or someone's cousin's mate would sit with her on the tube, leaning forward at first and then removing an earphone like –

Oh my god. Hi!

Wow yeah hello

And she would lean back and nod and raise a hand but they would hug her anyway

So what have you been up to?

Where did you go uni again?

Are you still in South London?

Yep.

I haven't moved either

Still in Tooting

You know I saw Miss Dawkins moved to Australia

Really

Yeah she got married and moved to Australia
Oh
And do you remember Eric in the year above he's got a baby now
Aw

But you weren't in my year were you
No.

You were in the same year as those twins that got expelled
Yes
I wonder what happened to them

It was you and that girl, what was her name she was so tall
Jade
Yeah, Jade.

And what about
Yep
What about
Yep
What was his name
Yep
Leo.
Oh
What about Leo
Um
What's he up to? Is he alright these days?
No we're not in touch. We're not in touch.

I saw him the other day
Yes.
He had a broken arm
Oh
Poor guy his arm was broken

Look I'm getting off here –
Oh but it was good to see you
Yes
I'm glad you're alright
Yep
Take care
Yup
Take care of yourself
Yes
Take care
Yep yes. You too

She ran a bath.

In the bath she put her face under the surface and shut her eyes. She held her breath until the hot water filled up her ears.

But now she was back.

What had happened was she had come back home. Had sunk back into this city that was warm too dark and always winter.

On Friday nights she had stopped drinking drinks with double doses. The older people from her work went for pints in the evenings on Friday. They kept going in the booth that they always booked out and they never realised how pissed they were until they stood up. They kept going until it was time to get McDonald's.

When she went she did the thing where you get a soda water but ask them to put a lemon and a straw in it so it looks like a G and T. She never stayed late. The night bus traffic through Clapham made her feel too nauseous. I'm so sorry but I've just got to get the last tube home! South London, you know. She played tetris on the empty tube. English people drink too much anyway. Slot slot slot slot.

On Saturdays she always meant to exercise or wake up at the same time and leave the bed and leave the house to see an exhibition or read a book or at least walk the dog with her dad or go shopping to Sainsbury's with her mum.

But on Saturdays somehow she always ended up losing her phone or her charger in the house under the sofa or under a pile of coats so she missed all her messages, although often there were no messages. She watched whole series in one go on her laptop and when the characters died she felt a real hollow sadness and when they committed moral transgressions she felt dirty and anxious and sweated into the sheets. And even though she hadn't done anything, she couldn't tell where the day had gone, she hadn't showered or anything the whole day it got dark so quickly, she didn't sleep and kept getting more fuzzy and more tired and didn't end up falling asleep until late too late. Sometimes late late in the night when she was feeling fuzzy tired she would look at the photos online.

(Do you remember what his flat looked like in winter all dark grey with the lights off?)

In the afternoon her dad called her from downstairs. She could hear her dad calling her from downstairs. She was quiet.

And then, from halfway up the staircase, her mum said her name. And again.

And then –

Vovó and vovô are on Skype

Oi oiii oi

Can you hear us?

Do you want to come down?

She didn't say anything. She heard her mother tread tread slowly up the stairs until she stood on the other side of the bedroom door.

Her mum spoke in a low voice with pauses –

Vovó and vovô are on Skype

Darling?

They are going in a minute

Do you want to say hello?

She didn't say anything. She was awake. She lay still. She didn't say anything.

She waited without speaking until she heard her mother's socks shift on the carpet. She heard the voices on the other side of the laptop screen.

She must be asleep, next time.

Yes she works very hard and she gets very tired.

You know what young people are like they can sleep forever.

Her mother began to move down the stairs.

The light from outside the curtains spread over her eyelids like concrete.

Jade was coming for roast. That Sunday Jade was coming for roast. Her mum had said the week before – Why don't you invite Jade over? And her dad had said – Yes, it would be great to see Jade! What is she up to now?

When she woke up on the Sunday morning that Jade was coming for roast she had a shower straight away and did not go back to bed. She put on a clean vest, soft trousers that didn't pressure her stomach, and moisturised her face. In the late morning she went downstairs and sat at the table with her parents as they prepared the meal.

Good morning

Good morning!

Her mum was peeling potatoes.

Vovó and vovô called on Skype yesterday.

Oh?

But you were asleep.

Oh.

We did not want to wake you.

Thanks.

She sat at the table.

How are they?

Good. Good. There is a new tree in the garden

Oh?

Jabuticaba

Oh.

You know it is the small black almost black fruit

I know it. She paused. That's nice.

Yes.

She looked at her dad.

Her dad smiled at them. I've got a *large* chicken because Jade is coming today.

Yes.

Her mum looked at her. Jade is coming today, yes?

Yes. She got her phone out of her pocket. Yes she texted me this morning.

They looked at her.

She said she should arrive at one o'clock.

Great.

Great.

Her mum was staring at her.

Mum?

Sorry. Her mum restarted peeling the potatoes.

Her dad was doing something important at the stove. In response to no one, he said – Yes. Food should be ready at about one fifteen.

She put a piece of bread in her mouth and watched them from her side of the table.

They made this meal together every week, every Sunday just the same since she had been a child. But it was her dad's meal really. Her mum peeled the potatoes and made sure there was enough ice cream to go with pudding. He bought and chose the vegetables, which always included parsnips and swedes and marrows and other turnip things that only grew in England. And he prepared the chicken. Today with butter and pieces of garlic and – I'm experimenting here folks, so let me know if you notice anything different! – a lemon inside.

When she was growing up it had been unusual for them to eat the roast just the three of them. Her mum had always found and invited some random Brazilian nurse or new doctor from the hospital who had always brought their partner or sister or daughter who was wearing a fleece, visiting Europe for the first time. Or there was one of their cousins, or cousins' cousin, visiting from Manchester or Bristol or São Paulo. A house like this should be full of people, her mother had said, although recently it had only been the three of them.

The doorbell rang.

I'll get it.

She closed the kitchen door and stopped for a moment in the corridor. She could see the shape of Jade on the other side of the stained glass front door.

Jade came from the dark grey late winter into the kitchen where all the window wall was steamed up.

Hello!

Hello

Jade! Her mum removed her glasses and stood up and gave Jade a hug — You look so beautiful and grown up Jade.

Aw thanks. Thank you.

Her dad looked up from the gravy and shook Jade's hand.

Oh hullo Jade!

Hello!

And the dog also wanted to sniff her tights and sniff her handbag.

They sat down around the table. Jade had arrived a little early.

We're not *quite* ready yet Jade.

Oh don't worry —

Would you like a glass of wine?

Yes! Thanks.

All ready on the table was a tray of goose-fat crunch crispy potatoes and carrots and onions and parsnips, cabbage in a dish, water, wine, wineglasses. The fruit bowls and flower vase were pushed to the sides of the table around their plates.

They sat around the table and looked at each other. Her dad poured the gravy into the gravy boat and handed it to her mum, who set it down on a mat.

Her parents were embarrassing her.

Jade, so tell me have you graduated?

No, next year

Ah well good luck good luck.

And your degree will be in — what's the name exactly?

Fine art.

Oh right and what does that, you know

Well I did like films and sculpture, sort of both at the same time sometimes

— Jade's work is great.

Her mum said — Yes I would love to see it, we always want new pieces for the hospital

Mum —

What?

Obviously it's not like that — how would you put a film

What do you mean it's not like that, why not, Jade you could make something for the hospital

Yeah I suppose I could!
Anyway
Jade have you got gravy there

They passed around the gravy boat.

So what kind of job will you have?
Well right now I work in a cafe but
I mean do you know what kind of thing would you like to do?
I'm not sure yet.
You could always keep up your art
Yeah I
Jade, would you like more chicken?
Jade held out her plate. She turned and said —
But anyway how is *your* job?
Yeah! Good, they renewed my contract.
Amazing.
Yeah
I'm so happy for you

Her dad said — It was a really hard-hitting programme about plastic surgery in Brazil.

She looked at her dad.

Her mum looked up too.

Jade looked at her — Cool.

No I mean, it was — she was flustered — it was like the presenter was English, you know she's the um the blonde lady with the fringe from um I forget what she was called, but anyway it was her and she had various theories about the whole thing.

Like she asked the women if they were doing it for the husbands

Right

They said no, most of them didn't even have husbands

Right

Jade was listening.

Looking at the wall behind Jade, she winced — And then the presenter said, did they want their noses to look less African? She asked them if they voted and they said, yes and voting in Brazil is compulsory. She said, why didn't they go to the gym or run on the beach instead

Jade frowned.

Afterwards they loaded the dishwasher and her mum took the little pudding plates and little forks out of the cupboard.

Your father has made fruit salad, it has a little rum in it. And there are two types of ice cream, this one with strawberry bits I think is a bit fancier the other is just vanilla.

This is lovely thank you

Yes you can get very ripe fruit at the market

Mmm

Are these lychees?

Yes. Yes they are lychees.

They ate.

How is your mum Jade?
She's good. She's on holiday right now.
And Andy?
Also good.
Does he still work at the council?
Yeah. Yep he does.
Right.
Yes.
Well do send my regards to them.
Yes.

Still sitting at the table, Jade asked her – Do you want to go to the cinema?
Her parents were moving around the kitchen, stacking plates.
I don't think –
Elena's going.
I have a thing
We're going to watch the scary one –
I have a thing I have to do.
Okay.
Sorry.

If it had been summer perhaps they might have sat in the garden together.

Before Jade left, they hugged by the coats in the doorway.
I'll see you soon though.
Definitely.
Yes

Jade smiled at her. Okay then.
Bye
Byebye

And then after the front door shut and outside started getting dark she sunk down into her bed with relief and opened the computer, typing in the letters of his name.

Do you remember what his flat looked like in winter all dark grey with the lights off?

Do you remember what his flat looked like in all dark grey covered in two hundred tiny candles?

Because — be honest with yourself

There were good times

(yes)

Hey!

Hey

Hey.

Hi

Hiya

Hello!

Hello

It's me

I know it's been a while but

Leo —

She didn't tell anyone this but walking home from the N155 bus stop, on a night when she had actually been out drunk a couple of drinks, walking home from the bus stop as she crossed the high street she heard a voice call her name.

She heard the

syl
la
bles

Felt her whole body thrill unthrill

She heard the

syl
la
bles

She kept walking, her back to the nighttime name sound.

(Of course it wasn't him
  she'd *know* the voice)

She kept walking
It was dark and

this was a new coat these shoes were new boot shoes; she wore no evidence of herself as he had known her on her body

She kept walking swish swish swish

(Of course it wasn't him
    she would *know* the voice)

She turned the corner –

ran.

Yes she was back.

The next weekend on Saturday she went shopping with her mum. They drove to the big Sainsbury's in Tooting Broadway.

But

Her mum held up little yoghurt pots – Sugar free? No? Do you prefer honey or mango? Do you still like lentils?
　No
　Yeah
　No
　Mum –

But

Two roads from the entrance – she knew the spot. She had spent probably over three hundred evenings there. In the maisonette garden. Every time she was watchful in the Sainsbury's. Checked the shoppers in all directions. Tall light hair slim fingers? Black jacket football shorts, his naked back.

　Darling will you go to the freezer section please?
　We need peas and ice cream and prawns little prawns shrimps
　And can you think of anything else
　Her mum bent over the trolley.
　She shook her head.

She took a bath. Filled it full and hot and covered it in bubbles.

She took off her blazer and her blouse and her tights and her other clothes. Got her whole body in the bath. Didn't look at it.

this broken body

this broken up body.

She wakes from a bad dream

It was true she checked his Facebook. She had thrown away all her shiny paper photographs of him at some point she must have done it, she couldn't remember when, including the tiny ones they had taken in the photo booth at the station in Brighton. To be honest she had been checking his Facebook. She checked it more now that she was back home. These had been their places after all. Although unlike her, he had never left. She had never gone back right up to the door of his flat. Although somewhere, in some drawer, she had the key (and the other day for the first time in years she had held it in her hand again)

She almost called Jade almost saying I had a dream where he had broken his arm

In her sweaty sheets childhood bed she looked through the pictures on his Facebook, the ones that she had access to. He didn't upload new ones often. So she couldn't tell if he was happy or sad or where exactly he was living.

A photo of him by the sea
A photo of him with some dog in a living room she didn't recognise
A photo of him in a bedroom she didn't recognise
A photo of him wearing blue scrubs like on TV and smiling
A photo of him broad shouldered in a suit
A photo of him with new glasses, his hair cut shorter than she had liked it.
A photo of him by the sea

Every time, she cringed when she saw his face, its shocking unrepeatable asymmetry. The way it shouted out to her in his voice. We used to fuck, his white body said to her as it stood by the sea, you used to fuck my mouth.

He crouched in the living room she didn't recognise. His asymmetrical smile. Under all the clothes in all his photos she saw his naked body.

White like a glowworm.

But there were good times
There were good times. Come on. Be honest with yourself.

Yeah the sex had been good sometimes.
    You called it great
    I know.

You called it —
    Sometimes it was ugly.
    But still

And she had loved him.
    Yes.
    And he had said — If you love me don't you leave me

    (if you love me)

And there were other things. But she's a stubborn archivist.

Tall light hair slim fingers

his white and naked back

And unlike her, he hadn't left.

Had he?

Hey — I recognise you
Yes
What's your name?

He repeated the syl-la-bles.

Yeah that's nice, where's it from?
It's from Brazil.
Jeeeez. He bent over and whistled.

And you kissed his face all over every single part of his white paper no face face, cheek and ears and teeth and mouth and mouth and you almost bite it off and chew

Hey!

Hey

Hey.

Hi

Hiya

A photo of him, by the sea

Hello!

Hello

It's me

I know it's been a while but

And I'm sorry

Jade I need to talk about –

She wakes up from a bad dream

a face seconds above her face a white face above her face

It was bound to happen

And she didn't tell anyone about it but she had heard a voice call her name

She ran home and sat on the toilet, shitting, sweating, her face in her hands.

PART II

1991

Natal

THE FIRST TIME Ana Paula came to England was to see her sister's baby.

It was her first time on an aeroplane and her first time over the wide grey ocean and the first time she used her passport.

It was the first time Ana Paula left Brazil.

Isadora was sitting on the sofa in the living room in their small flat in Tooting in the late morning. She was breastfeeding and trying to eat mushrooms and tomatoes and bacon and toast from a plate on the coffee table. Richard was in the kitchen, and Isadora could hear his kitchen movements as he made his own breakfast plate.

Richard came into the living room.

Without looking up she said — Their plane arrives at one.

He nodded, eating.

They land at one.

Yes. Yes.

Then, looking at the sky in the window, he said — Yes, they must be somewhere over France at the moment. Near the Pyrenees I would imagine.

Isadora did not respond. She took a bite of mushrooms and mushroom-soggy bread. The second bedroom was made. The heating was on, the flat was warm. Ana Paula would have to sleep on the sofa but there was nothing they could do about that. When her parents had first responded to her letter they had offered to stay in a hotel but she had said, over the phone, No no claro que não. Imagina.

Isadora looked at the baby then back at Richard — She is still hungry.

Richard paused. Well —

Well?

Richard sat next to Isadora on the sofa and put the side of his hand on the baby's head. Well, I could go to the airport and you could stay here — with the baby.

Isadora considered. Isadora shifted.

You go pick them up on your own?

Yes.

Isadora shifted. The baby made a small sound.

Then she said, slowly — I think they will really like that.

Great.

Great.

Richard looked at Isadora.

She smiled at him. Thank you husband.

But — she said — but in case you don't recognise each other, just in case, let me make you a sign.

Isadora handed him the baby and moved the breakfast plate. She took a piece of white A4 paper from a pile of letters on the coffee table. On the back of it she wrote, first in orange highlighter then traced over in black biro —

AMADO

(Vovô, Vovó e Tia Ana Paula)

She stood and held up the sign.

She was laughing — Okay?

Richard looked at it and then he frowned.

So what do I call them — Mr. and Mrs. Amado?

Isadora repeated, in a Deep English Voice — *Mistuh und Missus Uhh-maar-doe*

He chuckled. (Richard could laugh at himself.) So I'll call them Voh voh and *Voh voh*?

He held the baby out to her but she was still laughing.

Just call them Cecília and Felipe. And Ana Paula.

Really?

Really. She handed him the paper and took the baby back.

It's not very formal.

I know. But it's intimate.

Right.

And that's what we're going for.

Intimate.

Yes.

Yes.

There was a pause. Isadora could tell that Richard was nervous. As the baby breastfed she leant forward and restarted eating her breakfast. She looked at Richard.

Husband –

Yes?

Go.

And there he was. At one o'clock. Englishman Richard from the photos! And there was Richard, tall narrow nosed blue eyed corduroy Richard, safeguarding two trolleys with his limbful body by the metal barrier at the arrivals section of Heathrow Terminal 3.

Richard! Re-shar-de, whose name they imagined in italics.

The three greeted him with over-formal over-pronounced English, two sets of kisses and a handshake.

He was so glad to meet them!

Kiss kiss!

They were so glad to meet him!

Kiss kiss!

Isadora was at home with the baby –

The baby!

Had they had a good flight?

The car was in the carpark –

Welcome!

How was their flight?

We're so glad you've come for Christmas, yes!

And the plane food was alright?

Yes it is quite chilly here!

There's lunch for us at home

No no let me take that Cecília you must be exhausted

Richard led them through the glass doors onto the airport street in the direction of the carpark.

Vovó Cecília walked into the skin-pricking greyness with her hand resting on her husband's arm. She had brought gloves. She took them out of her handbag and pulled them over her hands and fingers. She was wearing kitten heels and face powder with maroon lipstick and a light blue two-piece with shoulder pads. Her husband was wearing a thick brown tweed suit and matching hat. Despite their curiosity, Vovó Cecília and Vovô Felipe walked a few paces behind their son-in-law.

Ana Paula walked a few paces behind them.

She was concluding that Heathrow Terminal 3 was ugly. It had low ceilings and too narrow corridors and long queues at passport control. But it smelt clean, and cold, like the English word "crisp." (Which she knew could also mean "potato chip.")

Ana Paula felt the cold quiet under her feet and against her face.

Much like the building, Richard was underdressed. But Ana Paula, who had seen one photograph of her brother-in-law, already knew that she liked Richard. And Ana Paula liked Heathrow Terminal 3.

As they approached the car, Vovô Felipe began — The timing is good, the timing of this visit is very fortunate. We want our daughter Ana Paula to see Europe before she begins university.

And so the great reconciliation happened like this (it had in fact begun six months before with a letter or a transatlantic phone call and the news of a difficult pregnancy) after ten years on different sides, and five years on different continents, this tall pale greyblue eyed probably a socialist English man, who their daughter had married at a wedding to which they had not been invited, would drive Vovô and Vovó Amado in his cold brown Volvo down the dirty A4 and then through Fulham and across the river to their eldest daughter.

He also drove Ana Paula.

That evening was quiet. Vovó Cecília and Vovô Felipe were tired but they kept their shoes on. They thought the flat, which was up a set of stairs on the top two floors of a terraced house around the corner from Tooting Broadway station, was shabby, but they said nothing. It was not an apartment but a part of a house. There was only one bathroom.

Richard made his bay leaf and mustard and secret ingredient spaghetti bolognese and they ate together in the sitting room as the baby slept on a blanket on the floor. Vovó Cecília could see the baby, hear the baby, hold the baby.

The baby
The baby who, wrapped in blankets and socks and coats, became starfish shaped
The baby who Richard wore like a backpack when he went to Sainsbury's
The baby who Isadora had spent thirty-six hours in labour for
The baby who was breastfed constantly
The baby who people said looked like Richard narrow nose round eared Richard
The baby who had been born small, a little on the small side
The baby who
The baby who was wriggle wriggle moving and entirely alive.
The miracle baby who didn't cry
Baby pink, baby green, baby yellow
The first baby in the Amado family since Ana Paula
Baby

After eating, as Isadora loaded the dishwasher, Vovó Cecília, who remembered the two miscarriages and one stillbirth between her first and second daughter, looked at the glowing wriggling baby in awe.

Richard was also looking at the baby.

She said to Richard – She is beautiful.

I know

She has light eyes like you

Yes, yes she does

Beautiful

Yes

And look at her delicate nose

Before bed, at the end of the evening, Vovó Cecília held the baby on her lap (the baby against her face, the baby rocking in her arms).

The flat was warm and quiet and full of the orange yellow of indoor lamps. Vovó Cecília was in the bedroom with the baby. Richard was on the phone in the kitchen to a colleague at the hospital and Vovô Felipe had gone to sleep.

Ana Paula sat in the living room. Isadora held up a sheet and pillow and duvet to go on the sofa.

Ana Paula, this will have to be your bed.

Yes.

I hope that it's comfortable.

It will be.

Ana Paula made her bed. Isadora watched her.

Isadora leant on the side of the sofa. The living room was covered in small blankets and wipes. She began to clear it for Ana Paula.

Mumãe is so good with the baby, no?

Ana Paula nodded. Mmn. She is very happy.

Isadora looked away.

It is a relief –

Richard looks just like the photo.

Ah

Isadora looked at her sister.

He likes to cook?

Yes. Yes he is very good at cooking.

Ana Paula nodded. She had finished making the bed.

Ana Paula sat over the sheet on the sofa. She moved her bare feet under the duvet. Isadora sat down opposite her, sliding her feet under the other side of the duvet. It was not cold but outside of the bay windows was dark.

Isadora waited for her sister to speak.

I hope I can say, but you look so grown up and like a woman.

Ana Paula wrinkled her nose and mouth and didn't look at Isadora.

Under the duvet, Isadora moved her feet.

I am happy you are here.

Ana Paula looked at her sister but didn't speak.

There was a silence.

You were gone a long time –

You look so grown up –

Ana Paula said to her sister – Do you remember the year that you left home, running around the supermarket listening for the sound of the price labelling machine? Remember it was because the price was increasing by the hour and we were trying to get to the food before it got relabelled. We used to go with Dona Antônia.

For a few seconds Isadora didn't respond. Then she put her hands around her sister's toes. Because Isadora could remember being nineteen and seeing her big toothed pre-pubescent sister running through the supermarket aisles in blue shorts and lace up shoes.

Que saudade de você.

Ana Paula opened her mouth but didn't say what she was thinking.

Once she heard the two bedroom doors close, Ana Paula changed into her pyjamas. She folded herself into the foreignness of the duvet, its muted smell. Like a small animal, she poked her head and fingertips out of the duvet. She turned the television on without the sound.

She stared behind the television through the first floor bay windows of the flat. Ana Paula was thinking that her sister had changed in the years since she had last seen her. Isadora wore her wavy hair short like a boy and had a new rounder mother shape. Her face was whiter and her glasses had thinner frames. She had been wearing a loose floral dress and woolly socks that unrolled over her calves. Ana Paula would say she looked more English, except Isadora didn't look English at all.

Outside, Ana Paula heard the sound of heavy suitcase wheels bump bump thump across the pavement slabs.

By the moving light of the ten o'clock news, Ana Paula surveyed the two whole walls of bookshelves from under the duvet.

Emily Brontë
George Eliot
A. S. Byatt
Margaret Atwood
Toni Morrison
James Baldwin
Emily Dickinson
Salman Rushdie
Clarice Lispector
Camões
Jane Austen
Jane Austen
Jane Austen

One Portuguese grammar book
A wide photo book of Picasso paintings
A Winston Churchill biography
Marx
Lenin
Engels
Dostoyevsky
Tolstoy
Shakespeare
Shakespeare
Shakespeare
a complete shelf of ripping Agatha Christies.

Ana Paula knew about half of the names and had read perhaps five of the books she saw. She read in big white letters "Zola," and she imagined it was another one of those stories about an aristocratic woman, like *Anna Karenina* next to it. It was unlike their living room at home, from which she also watched the news broadcast from the BBC red desk. The Amados had one bookcase, featuring most prominently big brown dictionaries and encyclopaedias. Ezra Pound, she thought, would be a good name for a female boxer.

Ana Paula had not been naive enough to expect snow; but the cold wet outside viewed from the dark dry inside, the conical sheets of yellow rain under the streetlights, the precipitation that brought no rising smells and that bit your fingers, the vast smallness of everything — the little square hedges with little privet leaves, the hip-height walls, the patterned windows under corniced arches, the narrow brick houses, the curved streets, the understated use of concrete — was almost overwhelming to her.

For hours that night Ana Paula basked in the rightness of this cold Christmas.

Outside, she heard the sound of heavy suitcase wheels bump bump thump across the pavement slabs.

On their first day all together Vovó Cecília and Isadora had breakfast late in the kitchen with the baby. There was fresh bread — real pão francês — and scrambled eggs with cheese and ham and oranges and cloudy apple juice.

Vovô Felipe read the English newspaper in the armchair by the window in the living room. Richard sat next to him on a kitchen stool and read a different section of the paper.

Richard, what does your sister do?

Richard looked up from his paper — My sister? She's a biology teacher.

In a public school?

Yes, in a state-run school. She was recently made head of the biology department.

So you are a scientific family.

Richard paused. Yes. Yes, I suppose we are.

Ana Paula will study law at the University of São Paulo, the best university in Latin America.

Oh! Fantastic! Yes, Isadora mentioned it to me.

Yes, and law is one of the most competitive degrees. Apart from medicine.

So in the university where Isadora studied?

Yes, it is. And it is where I studied, and my brother Henrique, and my father, who was one of the first dentists in the state of São Paulo.

Richard nodded.

One time Richard, I will tell you the story of my father.

Richard looked briefly at the newspaper.

Richard, Isadora has told me that you are from Yorkshire, in the north of England.

Yes. I grew up just outside Halifax, and my parents still live there.

And are they also doctors?

No. My dad was a school teacher and my mum stayed at home.

Isadora has told me that you studied for your medical degree in Manchester.

Yes, I lived there for seven years.

It was the great centre of the industrial revolution.

Yes, indeed.

Vovô Felipe folded his paper.

I have always liked England, it is an *illustrious* country with ancient, respectable institutions and noble statesmen and writers.

Oh?

Vovô Felipe was nodding. I have always said that Brazil would have been better off if it had been discovered by the British. The Portuguese, they did not do a good job in terms of infrastructure and culture — we are not so sophisticated, you know —

Vovô Felipe leant forwards and looked at Richard.

Have you ever visited Australia? No? Ah but Australia is a very advanced country, although it is just as hot and tropical as Brazil, comparable in terms of ecology and climate and indeed coastline. We would have been like Australia, a tropical country also, but colonised by the British.

Richard's hands were on his thighs, but he stayed sitting. Oh.

Vovô Felipe continued, pointing at the paper — Richard, it says here that the Queen will make a speech on Christmas Day.

Oh. Yes. She gives a speech every year.

It will be played on television.

Yes.

And will you watch it?

Richard paused. I don't usually watch it.

Vovô Felipe nodded.

And it is true that many English families do watch it. But — Richard paused — But I thought we might go for a walk instead. A Christmas Day walk is also traditional in England.

Vovô Felipe nodded.

We're in the city of course, but we could go to the common.

Richard looked at his father-in-law.

Ana Paula stood up and left the room.

Later that day, when Isadora was dressed and the baby was asleep and with Vovó Cecília, Isadora asked her husband a question — Richard, do you need vegetables? Are there vegetables that need to be bought?

Yes! Yes, there are indeed vegetables to be bought — all the shops will be shut early tomorrow on Christmas Eve, and even then, even before then, the best ingredients might run out.

Richard opened the fridge door.

And as well as potatoes and parsnips and brussels sprouts, we need tin foil and cloves.

Isadora leant in to kiss her husband on the cheek.

She looked at her sister. She said — Richard, make a list and I will go with Ana Paula. The baby is asleep.

She put her shoes and coat on and looked at her sister.

Late much later in the day, when it was dark, the two returned with full bags.

That took a while, did you have trouble finding everything?

You are so late! It is so cold outside!

Isadora looked at Richard and then at her mother — But it has been ten years.

She looked at Ana Paula.

But it has been ten years.

And so, the great reconciliation happened like this, with presents and a ceia the Brazilian way on the 24th on Christmas Eve —

White baby dress
Pink slippers in pink wrapping paper
Green flowered hair clips even though the baby had no hair

Roast turkey, of course
Richard wearing oven mitts

A pair of matching maroon gloves and scarf
A book on the origin of English proverbs

Goiabada, doce de leite, bis chocolates, more pão de queijo mix

A too wide pair of blue swimming shorts
A thin green cashmere jumper (I tried to get one that would be thin enough to wear in São Paulo in the winter)

Goose-fat crispy roast potatoes
Peas in mint and butter
Roast carrots and parsnips
Gravy
Richard wearing oven mitts

Chopped cucumbers, lettuce, tomatoes chopped slowly by Vovó Cecília who didn't know how to negotiate a manicure with a chopping board and knife and vegetable juice.

Brussels sprouts and a little garlic

Stuffing
Gravy
Gravy is? Gravy is, like a meat juice or a sauce, how would you say gravy

A pair of flower earrings for each of the daughters
A woolly jumper for Richard

Brazilian rice with raisins in it
A chocolate cake with the doce de leite icing from a special recipe that Isadora had asked Ana Paula to ask Dona Antônia to write down.
Christmas pudding
Brandy butter
Pão de queijo (why not?!)

A stuffed animal called a tamanduá
(the baby asleep and wrapped like a starfish)

Crackers
which Richard showed them how to use.

On Christmas Day Richard took his mother- and father-in-law on a walk. Yes my parents always go for a walk on Christmas Day. It is a traditional thing to do. We are in a city but

Richard took Vovô Felipe and Vovó Cecília to Tooting Common, strapping the starfish baby onto his front.

The long tall terraced house streets were very quiet.

Richard took them down the path by the frosted grass and showed them the woods cut in half by the train track and the rising mist.

Inside the flat, the sisters turned the heating up.

On Boxing Day Richard went to the common with Vovô Felipe again.

But Vovó Cecília stayed in with the baby because, really! The baby shouldn't be out in the cold again.

Que frio terrível
Querida netinha
O ano que vem o natal será na praia, no Brasil, que tal?

Isadora said — I'm going to take Ana Paula shopping.

We're meeting my friend Kalpana, we're going to Oxford Street, *Boxing Day sales* — Isadora said.

Not to be missed.

In some ways, the first time Ana Paula came to England, the timing was very good.

On Boxing Day, when Richard took Vovô Felipe out to the common again and Vovó Cecília had stayed in with the baby, the sisters had gone out. They put on innumerable layers of pants, long johns, vests, blouses, jeans, woolly jumpers, trackies, woolly hats, scarves and fleeces, raincoats, gloves and many socks. Isadora filled two bottles with milk and left them in the fridge.

We are going for our own walk now — Isadora had said.

Later later, when Richard was sitting in the living room with Vovô Felipe and Vovô Cecília, their wet gloves on the radiator, the baby asleep on a blanket, he got a call on the house phone from Isadora.

She said — We bought so many things and we ran into Kalpana, you know my friend from the hospital, and she invited us for dinner so we will be very late. Richard, will you tell my parents?

Richard —

She held the phone against her face.

You will be alright with the baby and my parents

This is what happened.

On Boxing Day they had gone back to the clinic where Isadora worked. Not to see Dr. Kalpana this time, but a second doctor.

Ana Paula sat down in the small white room with the second doctor who had said –

Well which is it, Ana or Paula? *A-nuh* or *Por-lah*?

And Isadora had said – It's Ana P*au*-la, *Ana Paula*, like Ka-*Pow* like *pow*-er

And then Ana Paula put the biggest most jumbo sanitary pad in her underwear and Isadora got them a cab, and when they were home while their parents were in bed Isadora ran her a bath and then wrapped her up on the sofa and Ana Paula put the news on with the sound off.

Suco de Cajú

DO YOU WANT to hear a funny story? A funny story about your father about your father's first trip here

Do you remember? No I guess you can't no no claro you were a little baby or maybe you were walking I don't know can't remember, can you remember? No of course not you were a baby.

We were all at the beach, you know like we always do, and we went for lunch in a restaurant, nothing too formal, one of those restaurants where they don't mind if you're wet from the beach as long as you have a shirt on or a canga round your waist, and you sit in plastic white chairs. Your father was sunburnt all glowing sea salt in his eyebrows his reading glasses on and trying to work out the menu in his rudimentary French. Batata frita, potato, frîtes — like that. We were staying in the little yellow house. You remember the yellow house? Yes yes obviously.

What happened in the restaurant was — and now that it's been explained to him he can laugh at it too but at the time — what happened in the restaurant was that obviously your father loves to cook, loves to garden loves planting plants — he would wander around the garden asking what was the name of this tree? Did anybody know the name of this tree? Was it a blublublabla? Insisting on sitting in the sun.

So your father every time we went out he would want to try a new juice. And obviously there are so many juices and fruits that he had never seen before

Açaí

Maracujá

Acerola
Jabuticaba

Cajú

He was always asking — But what is that in English? What is it like? Is it like a berry? How would you say "berry"?

So we were sitting in the beachside restaurant on the white plastic chairs holding the laminated menus, and he jumped in his seat, pointing at the menu, saying —

Soo-coh dee Kah-joo!

And I turned to him, and I turned to him, and said — Uh huh, suco de cajú, it's —

Juice

Yes

Juice of

Yes it is a juice

Juice of *cheese!*

Detective linguist your father was thrilled and outraged.

Juice of cheese!

Can you believe it? Oh it was very funny. At first not everyone had heard or understood what your father had said, and I was crying laughing hysterically, so your tia translated for them, and the whole table burst into laughter. The whole table was laughing, my sister, Vovó, Vovô, the family that owned the house next to the yellow house.

And all this time the waiter was waiting for us so when the waiter approached, pad in hand, and I turned to him and explained. And so he began to laugh too.

Your poor father this whole time was very perplexed, I put my hand on his shoulder and I said — No darling.

Queijo, like *kay*-joo is cheese.

And even then your father was still nodding, agreeing with me, saying — Yes. Exactly.

But cajú, like kah-*joo* is cashew fruit, like cashew nut in England.

Ah. So your father adjusted his glasses, looked around the table and then began to laugh. Poor husband.

No, but he found it very funny eventually when he understood what had happened. And he was so sunburnt. Your father can laugh at himself. Little lobster head.

1997

Vovó Cecília, A Love Story

DID YOU KNOW that your nails grow faster in the heat?

The baby looked at her nails.

The baby looked at Vovó Cecília.

They were in the Shopping. The baby had gotten too big to sit in the trolley and be pushed around, so she walked next to her vovó down the deep long high up aisles of sugar and flour and breads and baubles and cheese and shelves of nappies and shampoos lined with tinsel and the boxes of panettone and the boxes of panettone.

Vovó Cecília held the list in her hand.

We need sugar. It is over there can you get it?

Yes!

It will say A-Ç-U- with a little tail on the C

The baby frowned.

Bring back the middle-sized bag, not the small one or the very big one.

The baby ran down the aisle and brought back a middle-sized bag of sugar. She put it in the trolley. She looked up at Vovó Cecília — Next!

Okay — Vovó Cecília put her glasses on and held out the list — next we need butter. That's in another aisle where it's cold.

I know I know where that is!

Vovó Cecília clapped her hands.

Excellent! Lead the way.

The baby led them through the aisles past the eggs and the pasta and long legs of meat and the frozen pizza.

As they passed the fruit section Vovó saw the baby looking at the pyramid of grapes.

Let's get some grapes — would you like that?

Yes!

Let's pick a good bunch. Which do you think are the ripest?

Vovó paused to compare two bags.

The baby, her face much closer to the pile of fruit, touched one of the bags, knocking off a grape. She looked around and kept it in her hand.

I think these look the ripest. Do you approve querida?

The baby nodded.

They moved to the refrigerated aisle.

Butter!

The baby held the grape in one hand and the front of the trolley with the other.

Here here! Butter — M-A-N-T

She looked up.

Yes! You found it! Thank you querida.

Only — Vovó Cecília bent down to read the labels — only for the brigadeiros we need unsalted butter. Can you see if there is one that says sem sal?

Um

S-E-M S-A- —

The baby opened her mouth and then ran down the aisle away from the butter.

Vovó Cecília put her glasses on and began reading the labels.

A lady in the supermarket uniform approached Vovó Cecília. She spoke with a lisp because she was wearing braces although she looked about twenty-five. She held out a hand the same colour as Vovó Cecília's hand — Excuse me senhora can I help?

Ah yes, I'm looking for manteiga sem sal but I can only see salted here

Would that be for a savoury pie or a pudding

No no

Or for general cooking

No não I

And how much would you like, will you be cooking a lot with it? In your own house or at your —

I don't cook!

Vovó Cecília laughed.

The lady in the supermarket uniform nodded.

No I do not usually cook at all!

Vovó Cecília tapped her little heel shoe on the hard floor. She laughed.

No I do not usually cook.

Oh

But today, *today* I'm cooking brigadeiros with my neta.

Claro. I understand senhora

It is a special occasion. She has come all the way from London — which is in England — so I'm going to make brigadeiros with her. You can see her over there —

Claro

But it is an exception.

The lady from the supermarket looked over at the baby

The baby squished the grape into her palm.

I have a cozinheira who cooks for me

The supermarket lady closed her mouth over her braces.

Would you like me to get you that butter senhora?

Yes. Fetch it for me. Unsalted. *Unsalted.*

Unsalted.

Vovó Cecília looked at the baby, who was standing at the end of the aisle.

Yes because this section is very unclear and I do not have time to be running around.

Of course not. I am so sorry.

Yes you should rearrange this section.

We should.

It is badly organised.

Yes.

Please tell your manager I think it is badly organised.

I will be back in a minute with your butter.

Yes. Unsalted.

I'm sorry.

Well

Vovó Cecília pushed her lips together.

The baby, seeing the two women were no longer looking at her, put the grape in her mouth and wiped her hands on her top.

On the way back from the Shopping in the midday sunlight, as they waited for the big gate to lift so that Vovó Cecília could back into her garage, a woman in her forties wearing sunglasses and jeans and walking a poodle said — Senhora! Dona Cecília!

The woman tapped on the car window. Vovó Cecília wound it down.

Melissa! Bom dia.

Bom dia Dona Cecília!

Melissa, this is my neta I told you about her — from Londres!

Melissa said the baby's name like a question. She bent her body to look into the car, and smiled at the baby.

Melissa said the baby's name like an answer.

But of course I hear all about you!

Then looking up again at Vovó Cecília — Que fofa! Ai que linda! Aqueles olhos claros.

Vovó Cecília nodded.

How long is she here for?

Ten more days, we are going to the praia tomorrow. She is here in São Paulo just one more day.

Que pena. My nephews are about her age and they go swimming every day in the pool in their building.

Oh yes. What are their names?

Pedro Paulo and Roberto.

Oh yes, now I remember.

Next time.

Yes, next time.

Vovó Cecília called to the baby — Do you want to play with Melissa's dog?

And she speaks Portuguese?

The baby climbed into the front seat, where there was no child lock on the door, and let herself out of the car.

Yes claro, she speaks Portuguese.

The baby pulled the poodle's ears.

Yes my daughter visits every year so she speaks with us.

Yes! She looks just like your daughter. I forget is her name — Ana Paula!

No no não — she is not *Ana Paula*'s daughter!

No?

No, this is the daughter of my oldest daughter, Isadora. She lives in London with her husband who is English. She has lived there many years now. Yes you can tell because of the light eyes.

Melissa looked at the baby.

Lindos.

My daughter Isadora is a doctor, you know Melissa, and so is her husband. At a very large hospital in London.

Oh how spectacular

Yes

But it is hard. My only grandchild my netinha so far away, can you imagine?

What kind of doctor is your daughter?

Well

Vovó Cecília's house was on the slope of a hill in this city that was full of hills.

It was on a road that was all flat wide houses, looking out at the city that was all bars and blocks of concrete scraping the sky and turning from white to pink and grey in the pollution sunlight.

The house was wide with two low storeys. On each side of the house there was a high white concrete wall topped with triangles of broken glass that mirrored green into the top floor rooms. At the front there was a lawn thick with big bladed grass and enough space for two cars. Behind the house against the high white wall there was a second building that looked like it might have one or two rooms. Sometimes there were clothes hanging on the line outside it. The baby never went in there.

The front doors opened onto the big room with wide windows onto the garden. Around the windows the inside walls were white and covered sparsely with photographs, some in frames, all of them portraits. Some had more than one person in them but most of them did not.

In the middle of the room there was a plush cream sofa and on one side of it a small television and on the other side a dark wood dining table with a fruit bowl and another crystal bowl for sweets, and behind that a dark wood bookshelf holding the whole heavy *Encyclopaedia Britannica* set and leather-bound photo albums.

The baby had seen the pictures in the photo albums many times. They were the photos that the baby's mum had sent her parents, which lived also stacked in piles on shelves and in albums in London.

The photographs repeated themselves. Her, a tiny newborn baby, purple and eyes closed covered in cloth two hands almost the length of her body around her. Her, a set of little fingers reaching out of a pram, her father pushing the pram with one hand, then with much longer hair and hairy skinny legs propped out of shorts, the big jungle plants falling behind him, Kew Gardens, facing the camera. Her, oh my god face no front teeth by the snake enclosure at London Zoo. Tia Ana Paula, in a raincoat that didn't fit, standing outside Tooting Broadway station.

Her, on a swing in the playground by the tennis courts on the common, pink hood coming off, pigtails almost blonde, eyes closed in the air.

That afternoon they made the brigadeiros. There were only three ingredients and it would have been simpler to just start cooking and adjust as they went but Vovó Cecília used a recipe. It was handwritten in pencil in an A4 notebook. The baby looked at it and tried to follow but Brazilian handwriting was so curly it was hard to read.

They wore aprons, both of them white and pink and the baby's one going all the way to her ankles. Vovó Cecília rolled up the baby's sleeves and tied up the baby's hair. She arranged the unwrapped butter and opened cocoa powder and can of condensed milk on the kitchen counter. She got out a pair of scales and a big bowl. She put a chair in front of the counter for the baby to stand on.

I will read out the quantity and you will pour, tá bom?

The baby nodded.

200 gramas.

The baby gave the packet a tentative shake and cocoa powder fell out, filling halfway up the bowl.

The needle on the scale moved to 100.

The baby looked at Vovó Cecília.

Vovó Cecília nodded.

The baby poured in a little bit more cocoa powder and looked at the needle.

She poured in a little more.

And a little more.

She looked at the needle. And then she looked up.

Perfeito! Now we can start.

They had a gas stove that burnt gas from the big blue metal canisters that were delivered on a truck. Vovó Cecília lit the stove and put a pan on it. The baby stood in front of the stove on a chair and Vovó Cecília stood behind her.

You can help me do the cooking but you mustn't lean forwards over the fire, understand?

The baby nodded.

Vovó Cecília gave her a spoon.

Now put one spoonful of butter into the pan.

The baby put the spoon into the butter and then dropped the yellow lump into the pan where it began to melt.

Well done!

Now — Vovó Cecília picked up the pan and tilted it round — now I'm doing this part because it's dangerous. She moved her wrist and the butter slid all around the bottom of the pan and the sides until there was no spoonful lump left, just shine.

Have you got your spoon?

The baby held out the spoon.

Now I'm going to pour in the leite condensado and you're going to stir.

The slow thick leite folded into the pan and the baby ran the curve of the spoon deliberately around the curve of the pan.

Perfeito! Lindo! Keep going just like that.

The baby would have smiled but she was concentrating, using both hands to stir.

I'm going to pour in the cocoa powder now. Ready?

The baby nodded. Ready.

Vovó Cecília shook the bowl of cocoa powder over the pan and as the sprinkle powder became wet and fat and darkened the baby curved it into the centre of the hot leite condensado. And in stripes and strips the leite began to turn brown.

The smell of chocolate and hot condensed milk filled the kitchen.

Mmm! Is it making you hungry?

The baby nodded. Mmm hmm.

Me too.

The baby looked at her.

We need to keep stirring it right until when you pull the spoon back, until when you pull the spoon back like this – she put her hand over the baby's hand and drew the spoon to the side of the pan – until the leite holds for a couple of seconds and you can see the bottom of the pan.

The baby pulled the spoon back across the pan – Like this?

The brown folding sugar leite swelled up over the spoon as it moved.

No, not yet.

Okay.

Look – you can't see the metal.

The baby watched the pan, stirring.

When this is done, we will put it into a dish and leave it in the fridge so that it goes hard. Then we have to be patient again. Then comes the fun part.

But tell me if your arm hurts and I can take over.

The baby nodded.

She watched the liquid shift around the moving spoon.

Before dinner they sat at the table and Vovó Cecília put kitchen towels over the lace tablecloth and fetched the dish of set chocolate from the fridge. She also brought the unsalted butter, which she had left out and was soft, and a plate of crunchy sprinkles.

They sat at one corner of the dining table.

Vovó Cecília looked at her granddaughter — Have you washed your hands?

The baby held out hands that were damp but clean.

Vovó Cecília held out her own hands which had long elegant fingers with neat crisp nails painted dark red; also clean.

Me too.

Vovó Cecília put her fingers into the butter, scooped a digitful and spread it between her hands.

This is so the brigadeiros don't stick.

The baby nodded and did the same, rubbing the butter all over her fingers and palms and the back of her hands.

Agora do like this — she took a palm of the cold chocolate leite from the corner of the dish and rolled it into a ball the size of a two real coin in her buttery hand. She held out the shiny ball for the baby to see.

The baby nodded.

Now like this — she plopped the ball into the plate of sprinkles and rolled it around until it was covered.

Vovó took the squishy sprinkly chocolate ball between her pointer finger and thumb and put it in the corner of a new clean plate, where it sat expectant.

Pronto! Ready to do your own?

But the baby had already begun.

As the baby and Vovó Cecília rolled the thickened chocolate

into brigadeiros, a woman with dark skin wearing a hair net on the top of her head began to set the table around them. Vovó Cecília did not look at the woman, but the woman looked at Vovó Cecília. Looked at her butter shining hands.

Later, before bed, Vovó Cecília, the baby and Ana Paula sat on the plush sofa to watch the novela, the baby in the middle. This novela was set in Victorian times on a big farm in the North-East of Brazil and told the story of Bianca, a very beautiful sixteen-year-old with blonde hair that curled out of a bonnet, and a heart-shaped face and a heart-shaped mouth and huge brown eyes and breasts that rose in her corset when Aurélio, with whom she was desperately apaixonada, left and entered the frame.

Aurélio wore a necktie and boots and often had dirt on his hands. He was a modest young farmer who had recently come into money because of a tragic accident involving a cart horse. His neat jaw was covered in stubble and he had brooding eyebrows and a broad chest and thin falling ringlets of light brown hair.

Bianca and Aurélio's love was forbidden but often they found themselves alone — in the pantry, in the stables, against the door outside her father's study.

This time they were outside, walking through a sugar cane field as the sun set. The tall crop rose around them. Aurélio pulled Bianca close. She was almost crying, her mouth open. He leant in, as if to kiss her. She closed her eyes.

But I can never see you again, Bianca.

Aurélio!

I am sorry.

Aurélio held Bianca's chin in his hand, her tears falling onto his fingers.

He looked away from her. But I must go.

She held her hand out after him —

The interval music began.

Vovó Cecília stood up. The phone was ringing.

I'm going to see who it is, perhaps your mother.

Ana Paula and the baby sat on the sofa together.

Are you excited to see your mum and dad again?

The baby shrugged. Uh-huh. But — she held up three fingers — it's only been three days. That is not very long.

Ana Paula laughed. No? But you are very grown up.

The baby smiled.

And are you excited to go to the beach? The yellow house?

The baby nodded — I am! Yes!

What are you going to do there?

I'm going to swim in the sea, jump big waves, make a sandcastle, have an água de coco and an ice cream.

Me too.

Ana Paula nodded.

But only one ice cream?

The baby pulled a face at her.

They were quiet.

Then Ana Paula said — You don't have an empregada at your house in London?

The baby shook her head.

You have someone who babysits you and someone else who cleans but they only come some days and then they leave?

The baby nodded.

But if you and your parents lived here you would have an empregada.

Why?

Because you could.

At bedtime Vovó Cecília wrapped the baby in several thin blankets and kissed her face and told her a story. Sometimes it was the story of what had happened earlier in the novela or in another novela, or in a film for grown ups that the baby had not watched.

But today the baby asked for uma estória verídica. No it didn't have to be a new one.

The story began like this —

Once upon a time there was a girl who had just turned nineteen. She wasn't too tall or too rich or too beautiful but she was from an honest, hardworking family. She was the second of seven brothers and sisters, can you imagine that? She had big brown eyes and very straight teeth. Yes she was considered to have excellent teeth, and a lovely smile. Her name was Cecí.

Cecí lived in a city called São Paulo. Yes, she lived not too far from where we are now. She had finished all her schooling, and had come to live at her aunt's house. Her aunt was a very mean old lady. She was in fact Cecí's great-aunt. And the aunt didn't like Cecí and was always telling her that she was going to send her back to her father's house to live with all her brothers and sisters, which made Cecí sad and afraid. Cecí didn't think her aunt would really do it but she couldn't be sure.

Now Cecí had some friends in the city, her cousins mostly. They lived nearby and were all the same age. And together they did nice things like go to the movies and go for walks and in the evenings they got dressed up and went to balls, although her aunt was very strict and made sure Cecí was always back by ten p.m.

Now. The dresses Cecí wore to the balls were always very special and very beautiful, because her and her cousins were very good at sewing — everyone was back then because you didn't just go to a shop and get clothes that fit you, instead you went to the cloth shop, you looked at all the materials, then you chose the one you liked best and you could afford, and over days and days you made it into a dress for yourself. Making yourself a new dress could take weeks.

There was one ball that Cecí was especially looking forward to. She decided she would make herself the most wonderful dress. She chose two fabrics, one that was a kind of pale cream and one that was a dusty pink. For weeks Cecí would work on this dress. Cecí stayed up at night to finish this dress before the party, sewing and cutting and sewing in seams. The dress was tight around here — the waist — and long and layered after that and cream and pink and Cecí made herself matching gloves that went all the way up to her elbows. And gloves were not easy to make.

The ball was on a Saturday and Cecí finished the dress just in time on the Friday. So she wore the pink and cream dress to the party, ironed her hair and she wore the gloves to her elbows, and although lots of men asked her to dance they were all too short or too dull or too ugly and when she went home at midnight she hadn't met anyone she liked.

But

But

But one day the next week, in the middle of the day when Cecí was wearing her normal clothes, her hair barely cleaned and pressed and done properly, a lawyer came round to Cecí's aunt's house for dinner. The lawyer was helping Cecí's aunt with some problem she was having.

Now, not everyone thought the lawyer was good-looking. Cecí's aunt didn't. But Cecí thought he was exceptionally handsome. He was quiet and polite and had long eyelashes. And although they had dinner together, because she thought he was so handsome, Cecí said not one word to the lawyer! She felt very silly. She was sure he would not have noticed her.

But

But but but

The next afternoon, when Cecí came home from her errands, her aunt said that she had received an unexpected visitor at the house that morning. The lawyer! He had come to ask if he could take Cecí out for an ice cream and coffee on Monday.

Of course Cecí told her aunt to say yes. She was very nervous. She chose a nice dress, did her hair. But back then things were very different. Back then men and women weren't allowed to be alone together, so when Monday came Cecí's horrible aunty came for coffee and ice cream too! As a chaperone. Cecí was very embarrassed to have her aunt listen to all their conversation but still they spoke about Cecí and the small town where she was from and her brothers and sisters, and where he was from and his family and most of all Cecí thought that the lawyer was even more polite and good-looking than he had been at dinner.

And so they fell in love. The next Monday they had another ice cream and coffee, and the next Monday after that the lawyer came round for dinner. And when they were together they would talk and Cecí would stare at his long eyelashes and she would almost forget that her aunty was there.

After three months they got married. Although Cecí was nervous she was very happy because she loved the lawyer very much and because it meant that she wouldn't have to live with her aunt or her brothers and sisters.

They had a wedding and moved into their own little house in the big city.

And on the very first evening when they had their own house and Cecí was unpacking her clothes for the very first time, the lawyer her husband saw her white and pink dress and he said what is that for, and she said for balls. They had never been to a ball together so the lawyer had never seen Cecí's pink and white dress before. She told him that she had made it herself. She told him about the gloves that went to her elbows.

He said — I want to see you wear it.

So she put on the white and pink dress carefully and her new husband watched her. He did up the little satin buttons at the back and she pulled on the gloves all the way to her elbows, and her husband the lawyer with the long eyelashes told her she was the most beautiful woman he had ever seen.

In the night the baby dreamt in Portuguese.

The words fell around her brain bleeding like clothes in the wash —

the sound of Melissa
the sound of Melissa saying her name
the sound of Melissa who was a stranger saying her name

the sounds of it like hot water

Senhora –

Dona Cecília

Dona
Cecília

Cecí

amada

Cecí –
apaixonada

That morning, still on English time, the baby had woken up early. She sat in her room. Tried to unfasten the window. She opened the book she had and read a chapter.

Then she got out of bed. She opened the door of the wardrobe in her room. It was full of her vovó's clothes. They hung above her, so she touched them from below. She felt the hems.

She heard a movement in the corridor. She closed the wardrobe and sat on the bed.

She had breakfast with Vovô Felipe and Vovó Cecília. He was drinking coffee and eating a ham and cheese toastie. Vovó Cecília peeled a mango, cutting the mango meat into slices then handing the stone for the baby to suck on. (Later, she would hang the mango skin on a small plate under one of the trees in the garden for the hummingbirds.)

Vovô Felipe began –

Your mother has told me that you are already reading books.

The baby took the mango stone out of her mouth. I am!

That is very good.

You must also learn to read in Portuguese.

The baby frowned.

It is very important. But it doesn't have to be right now. Right now you can concentrate on English.

The baby sucked on the mango stone.

Portuguese is becoming an important language.

Later he would begin a history lesson –

Em mil quinhentos e

Pedro Álvares Cabral

Árvores what kind of árvores

Cabral cavalo cabrito

But Vovô I thought Columbus discovered America

No. Christopher Columbus discovered América do Norte.

América is a continent – two continents.

And Brasil is in América do Sul

There is also América Central and the Caribbean.

Let us look at the map.

That night she asked for another estória verídica. A different one.

Let me think.

Do you know about your vovô's vovô? He was a farmer many years ago. He had a small farm in a town by the edge of the jungle. Yes — like Aurélio.

And before he had come there had been nothing on the edge of the small town where it was very hot, just the jungle trees and plants and animals. Spiders and snakes and monkeys and fish in the river and onças all covered in spots. Onças!

When he had gone to live there with his brothers they had had to hunt for food some days, and chop down trees for wood to build their house and farm and they would get bitten by mosquitoes all night long.

If they needed something they couldn't get one of them would go into the market in the small town and trade something.

Over time their farm grew. They built fences and stables and coops and bought animals and bred other animals. They got two cows, and made milk and cheese. They got chickens for eggs and eventually they would plant corn in the fields. They had a goat but it was very badly behaved.

They built a wooden cage for the goat and some of the other animals. The brothers had become very strong by this point from carrying things around the farm. Like Aurélio.

Your vovô's vovô had in particular become very strong. And very good at hunting. He could always be relied on to go out and come back with a capivara or a fish or boar or some other animal that they could roast on the fire.

And one night he was gone and he came back with an onça!

Back then onças were much more common. They were the predators of the forest. You would never be allowed to hunt an onça now because of the laws but back then there were many onças in the jungle. His brothers woke up in the morning and there was an onça in the cage!

But they did not eat the onça. They might have made it into a carpet or perhaps they let it go back into the forest although they would have to be careful it didn't kill the cows.

But your vovô's vovô kept disappearing in the night.

And one morning he came back with a young índia. Because there were still índios living deep in the jungle.

No — they did not keep her in the cage.

The next day when everyone else had finished breakfast and they were alone the baby repeated this story to her tia Ana Paula.

Do you know it?

Yes. I have heard it.

Ana Paula frowned. But I do not think that is a real estória verídica.

Oh

I think — Ana Paula paused, searching for a word in English — I think that this story is just *bragging*. Like showing off. By vovô's vovô. I do not think it really happened.

Oh

These were the photographs on the wall —

A baby — her mother, Vovó Cecília's legs in the side of the frame.

A sixteen-year-old, her mother, smiling too broadly all her teeth showing, her face taking up all of the frame, her hair cut into an oval around her chin.

And one of them together around the same time, Ana Paula, a toddler in her mother's lap, both wearing dresses. A yellow wall behind them.

A child, this one was Ana Paula, you could tell from the black hair cut with a fringe, about four years old. Sitting on a chair, wearing a light pink dress with a white collar.

Ana Paula, her hair up in a bun with strands coming out, in long black clothes and eye shadow and lipstick holding a roll of paper, graduating.

Her mother standing, in a fitted dress, fifteen years older than in the other photograph, her dad with longer hair in a suit and smart shoes. Looking at each other but not facing, hands almost together, the flower beds outside Wandsworth Town Hall in the background.

Vovô Felipe, in a photo greyed with light a young man with fuller eyebrows in a white shirt and dark tie.

An ancestor who had Vovô's nose and a moustache, black and white and faded, not smiling, wearing a shirt and a tie and a hat.

Her grandmother with another face, skin softer lips darker face all in a white veil, her body in a white dress.

They were back in the Shopping. Just a few last minute presents and panettone. The baby loved panettone. She would be a grown up before she realised that it was not an everyday food or an originally Brazilian dessert and that it was not traditional to eat it soaked in milk.

The Shopping was huge. It was not like where they went shopping in Tooting. The carpark was massive with lots and lots of levels all hot and dark with the smell of petrol. The Shopping was not only where you went to buy clothes and presents and watch films, but also where you went to buy food and go to the supermarket.

They stood in the aisle with a trolley, the baby holding the front.

Do you remember where the panettone is?

I remember!

So lead the way!

She led them down the aisles past the bread and the piles of cheese and the long legs of meat and fridges.

Perfect!

The baby smiled.

Your mother asked for some things can you remember what they were?

Protetor solar

Yes.

They walked to the toiletries aisle.

Let's buy her shampoo too.

Did you know — Vovó Cecília touched the baby's left pigtail and then reached for the conditioner — did you know that your hair grows faster in the hot climate?

She brushed her granddaughter's forehead, her fingers beneath the hair.

They moved down the aisle.

Vovó Cecília touched her hand above the curve of her own wrist.

Vovó Cecília took a bottle from the shelf. The baby held her other hand.

She moved her lips together and looked at the baby's face.

A Casa Amarela

THERE WAS NOT always a yellow house here.

Did I ever tell you the story of the yellow house? No it was not always here. And did you know that it belongs to your vovó and not your vovô? Although yes of course you are right that they share their things. Yes of course — they both look after each other and share their things. They have been married for a very long time. But still the house came to them through Vovó and this is an unusual thing.

It was just a square of land that my mother inherited from one of her brothers. No I don't know why or how he had a little square of land there. Perhaps he had meant to live there or grow things or sell it but he never did. He was not rich. But it was not worth a lot of money. It still is not worth a lot of money. More now though but anyway

It was a square bit of land, and like the bit of land that you can see next door no one looked after it so it was covered in plants. The rainforest plants came back to grow there. Like the trees that have the car-sized troncos and the dangling skinny bendy brown tails, and what your father calls buttress roots, and low to the ground big leaf creepers, but then also the hibiscus and the banana trees and all the other plants from gardens nearby.

But it was not as overgrown as all that because when Vovó inherited it there was already a little house there. Maybe it was more of a shed in fact. It was the colour yellow. Bright bright amarelo in the sun.

We did not go there much when I was growing up. No it was

not comfortable like it is now. Vovô put the pool in when you were little — he said that you should learn to swim when you learnt to walk, and you did. There was not the house like it is now with shade under the big palm tree and the white tiles and the white plastic chairs and the air conditioning.

We did not go there when I was growing up — it was not a fashionable place. It was just a little fishing village with no shops and the same dirt road but what was different was the paved road that comes off the motorway, you know the one that leads to the dirt road, *that* road was also a dirt road then, I don't know if there was even a bus service. We went with friends to other apartments on other beaches, Guarujá, you know where Denise has the apartment

But I did come here when I was a bit older. After Tia Ana Paula was born. Older than you are now. I was a young woman. I drank beer sometimes with my friends that sort of age, I could drive already, which is how we got here. We used to fill up the car and drive down the estrada through the forest and tunnels and waterfalls down the dirt roads to the beach.

And it would be me and my friends, sometimes I would take boyfriends, yes I confess I had some boyfriends before your father — but they were not as handsome as he is. Look at him! It would not be possible. But some of them were very nice really. Although some less nice. Anyway, we used to camp on the beach or by the yellow house and swim in the sea during the day, some people would surf, and one time we were camping on the beach and in the night the tide rose and it started invading our tents. That was terrible everything became ruined and sandy

And to eat we could buy fish from the fishermen and fry them on fires that we made ourselves. And drink beer from the can. Yes, there were many many mosquitoes.

But it was very different then. When the roads improved Vovô decided to rebuild the little yellow house although of course it is still yellow. And there was the little ice cream sorveteria, with all the different fruit flavours and the tree that grew through the floor of the deck. Tia Ana Paula? I don't know if she came with her friends like I did. I was already living in England then. I do not know if she camped on the beach with her friends. You will have to ask her.

And you used to call it the casa amarela and then you would say — ama-yellow? To make sure that whoever you were talking to understood. You used to mix up the words in both languages to make sure you were always understood.

Oh it was adorable. You used to call it a casa amarela uh-mah-yell-oh? Not because you were confused but because you were making a joke. A lot of baby experts at the time back then used to say oh you shouldn't teach your child to speak in more than one language at once because it will confuse them blabla bla, but that is bullshit of course.

You were very adorable. It was a little joke. Maybe it was your first joke. Ama-yellow.

People used to bend down and ask the baby — aunts and uncles from her English family or sometimes English people who worked at the hospital — if she dreamt in Portuguese, which was a confusing question

amerelo
ama

amado
amarela

amar
amer
america

It was like asking if she ever dreamt about her vovó or Ana Paula or swimming in the sea or were they saying her name correctly

casa
casada
pedro árvores
casal

2010

The Goldilocks Zone

YOU ARE EIGHTEEN nearly nineteen years old and you make a friend with long and shiny biscuit yellow hair.

Hi.

Hi!

She big eyes smiles at you.

Everyone calls me Goldilocks.

She wasn't your usual type of girl friend, what with her tree-plotted generations of English *English* family and her pleasant pastures green upbringing. But she had liked you, handpicked you from the crowd on your very first day when you had stood quiet and unsure and a little bit aloof. You know, she studied languages and was so envious of people who spoke them at home, it is such a gift, isn't it, and she was definitely without a doubt going to raise her own children bilingual!

And on the second day she lifted you out of the crowd again and she insisted on taking you out for a drink — just the two of us, no I insist let me get this one! — for what was maybe the first time that a friend had ever bought you a drink.

You had sat in the pub like grown ups in the corner under the dark wood walls, and you ended up drinking a pint of ale without bubbles in it because she was drinking one and it seemed like the thing to do to say, I'll have whatever you're having! And she asked you about your mum and your vovó and your tia with her head on her hand and you stayed until past last orders and she really did listen to what you said and who wouldn't have been touched by that.

It was a beginning again. A place that was new and hallowed where everyone would be as smart as you and have read as many books as you and wasn't Vovô proud of you, did you see how he kept the photograph of you outside the library on the wall. This would be your taller adult life where you make your real adult life friends.

And you were new in that tiny city that you could walk across in an afternoon. Where people became confused when they heard your London accent and your foreign name and where you could go for weeks at a time and only hear English spoken on the street and where none of the other girls wore heels out dancing and the shops shut at five and you couldn't pay by card and shopkeepers asked you how you were doing and you couldn't even really go proper dancing and everywhere you looked it was the same people again and again and again.

Mum, I'm having the best time!

No no of course it's great, I love it! Of course I don't miss London I am really sick of London. Really fucking sick of —

You said it — to your mum and then yourself and then to everybody else — at first because it was true and secondly because you didn't want people to think you were a snob with your bob cut hair and your dark lipstick.

But look, Goldilocks was from the middle of nowhere and you loved her. Yes.

She even learnt to correct people when they said your name wrong. She intervened before you even flinched. And if that isn't friendship, what is?

People said that uni was all about sleeping around and getting really fucked and meeting boys or, if you really had your shit in order, finding a husband but for you it wasn't. Okay?

In the first and crowning summer of your friendship, which was hot and extra long because of global warming, she took you to a big midsummer party at her house, which was not only detached but surrounded by fields at the end of a narrow road with no street lamps. (But what happens if you want to order pizza?) To get there, you had to take a train and then another smaller train and then walk for half an hour.

She met you at the station — I can't believe you're here! You are here! I could have brought the car but it's so sunny, I thought, let's walk through the fields.

Her parents were very nice.

We've heard so much about you!

Yes welcome, welcome!

Hello

Please, there's cake and biscuits, but if you fancy something savoury or more substantial

Yes

And the weather is looking so promising

Yes

I am glad about the weather!

Yes.

There were siblings and siblings' friends helping to set up and wandering around the garden and the house. And her school friends and their parents and then some of the people they knew from university.

Would you like a cup of tea, a glass of water you didn't have to wait too long for the train did you?

Later, there would be punch and beers in ice and red and white wine and a barbecue that fed two hundred people. People came all in fancy dress and parked in the garden all three generations of everyone her family knew. Heels that got swapped for wellies. Wellies at a party! But the music went on late and was very loud — you could do that if you had no neighbours.

An old man with a moustache spun you around until he was sweating. And when the music changed two of her brother's friends began to talk very close very very close but she found you and emerged and holding a plate of food, she found you.

It was how you imagined the village parties in Thomas Hardy novels except with a pool.

At the end of the party, when the sun had risen and everyone was gone or asleep on the ground with their feet crossed by the bonfire, the two of you slept in her clean childhood bed, her elbows curling into your back.

And then.

You'd read all her Virgil (okay) and Dante (decent) and Donna Tartt (enjoyable) and she'd read the Zadie book that you gave her, and you'd both already read Margaret Atwood.

So it was time.

Let's do it!

Let's fucking do it!

I have the money, do you?

Yes!

Wait –

Yeah?

I've never been to South America before.

I know. That's okay.

Well . . .

Well?

I'm just going to call my parents.

Of course!

Okay!

It's an early summer evening, the sky ribbed white at ten p.m. You reach across the desk.

She looks up.

I can't wait to get out of here.

She smiles.

She slides her hand over and presses her fingers on yours. Her shining yellow hair fans across the desk, reaching for you too.

Before you go, you have a conversation with Jade, who you haven't seen in a while. It's getting warm and you're sitting in your garden.

So you think it will be fine.

I've known her for a while now.

That's true.

Jade pauses.

Don't you like her?

Jade pauses. No no!

Jade puts her hand on her other hand — I do. She's sweet.

She'll be polite with my family, that's her kind of thing.

Yeah. She is sweet.

And they'll love her cos she's a tall blonde European right?

Jade laughs.

Right!

So where did it go wrong?

Was it on the second day in the bar round the corner from your aunt's apartment when you're drinking beer for you and a caipirinha for her, and she repeats how well your aunt and her husband speak English, and if only her French could be as good! And you say, a little too quick, well they met at LSE.

Or is it when, after two days of driving up the coast, she looks pouting sad because nowhere is cheap enough. The feather bead necklace in the market wasn't cheap enough and the silver that couldn't possibly actually be silver wasn't cheap enough by half. You don't know what to say to her — We've arrived five years too late! There are no more dirt roads and the prices are almost like London and you say to her but this is Brazil. The São Paulo — Rio coast isn't cheap, it's where the middle classes go on holiday, it's the Hamptons.

What? She says. Where?

Or when you oil up on the beach and she tells you that you are causing irreparable damage to your skin.

My dad told me, and he's a doctor.

You lower your sunglasses.

You remind her that your mum is also a doctor. You ask her whether she thinks the guy renting out beach chairs has skin cancer, or the woman selling hats has skin cancer or the kids over there grilling cheese or the man surfing.

Or is it once you're driving, moving inland, and you get lost, and it's dark, and you ask her to wait in the car while you ask for directions and she runs out after you slamming the door and you know it's because she's too scared to stay there alone.

And when you turn around to tell her to *relax* you realise she's locked the keys in the car.

You shout — For fuck's sake!

For fuck's sake!

A man walking past stares at you.

God I'm a bitch, you think.

She looks like she's going to cry.

Or is it when she's flirting with that guy with the Che Guevara hair and when he goes to get her another drink she turns to you and says — He says I'm the blondest person he's ever met!

And you say — Yeah that makes sense.

But I thought you said Brazilians can look like anything?

They can. You point behind her — There's a blonde woman standing by the bar.

She shakes her hair, her head — But her hair is clearly dyed!

Um

There must not be many natural blondes in Brazil.

You put your drink down.

It's interesting actually because the word for blonde in Portuguese is loiro or loira, which I sometimes get called —

No no! But I would say you're brunette or olive or something

Yeah. So I guess what I'm saying is that "blonde" is a relative —

He says — she lowers her voice — *he says* that he thinks that Brazilian woman aren't as good-looking as everyone says either

Later as she curls her willow back into him you feel so irritated that you almost shake her and say — You are a fucking novelty to him, you know that?

Or is it when, at the end of the long silence after you ask her to wait in the car while you pee at a petrol station, she says — Well if Brazil is so safe then why do Ana Paula and Marcos live in a wire walled complex with guards?

Or maybe after that time on the penultimate day when you lock her in the car and she starts crying.

Or maybe it is fifteen minutes after your plane lands, when she emerges from the bathroom of the baggage claim hall in Guarulhos Airport looking all Nigel Thornberry in thin beige three-quarter lengths, birkenstocks, a loose white blouse and a khaki-coloured explorer hat that looks like it should have corks hanging off it.

You stare at her

You stare at the birkenstocks
You stare at her

> I need long sleeves otherwise I'll get sunburnt.
> Okay yes
> And I need the birkenstocks for ankle support.
> No no of course

But in your head, you baptise this look *colonial chic.*

A R— By Any Other Name

THE DOOR OPENS, and he comes in only a minute or two late. Even after all these years, he finds her immediately, catches her eye immediately. He puts his arm around her body and shoulder in greeting, his nose in the damp hair behind her ear that still smells of shampoo — Hello darling — and, leaving his scarf on the table, he walks to the bar. After a minute he returns across the room holding a glass.

He sits down, makes eye contact with her. She takes her hands from her lap and big white teeth smiles at him.

Cheers.

Cheers!

Thanks for coming.

No not at all.

She smiles at him.

He smiles.

I can't believe it. I can't believe you're here.

I know.

I can't believe I'm seeing you.

She nods. Me neither.

You look great. You look different.

Thank you.

He smiles. How are you?

Good. She opens her mouth. Great. I'm living here again. I have a job. Everything is —

She shrugs and nods and looks at him.

I'm happy for you.

But — she looks at him — But how are you doing?

I'm great. I'm working hard. Really hard. But it's what I've always wanted.

Great.

He smiles, bringing his hands together.

She looks at him.

He drinks.

Then she says — I think about you sometimes. In a white coat, holding a stethoscope

They both begin to speak.

Sorry —

No, go ahead, go ahead.

No —

She says — Go ahead.

He looks at her. How are your parents?

Good.

And how are all your friends? How is

Jade

Jade.

Yes, she's good too.

He puts his glass on the table.

She looks at him without speaking.

He pauses.

And —

She pauses.

He looks at her. Are you seeing anyone?

No. No. She shakes her head. No.

Are you?

No.

She nods.

I was. I did. For a while. But not anymore.

I'm sorry.

No — he shrugs — it was for the best.

Right.

She shifts in her seat.

It's different in here nowadays, isn't it?

Yeah.

So many people. A different type of people.

I know. It's nothing like when we used to come here.

I know.

It's nothing like what it used to be then.

She holds the edge of her chair under the table.

She looks at him.

But coming here, there's a lot to think about — I mean to remember

He moves his hands and looks at her.

Do you get that too?

He nods.

She nods.

She watches his hands on the table, thin fingers on the edge of the beermat.

Does it feel like a long time ago to you?

Does what?

She waves her hand — All of it. Does it feel like a long time ago to you?

He looks her in the eye — Yes.

She doesn't say anything.

He pauses — Yes.

She doesn't say anything.

In a good way I mean

He looks around and smiles, crossing his wrists on the table around his glass. He leans incrementally infinitesimally forward —

I really wanted to see you

I wanted to see you too —

I've been — I've wanted to see you to say something

He holds eye contact, his wrists crossing around his glass (her wrists crossing around her glass).

She looks away.

Do you remember — she says — do you remember, near the end, you know —

She looks away.

And her tongue sticks so he waits for her to begin again

I want to say something, you know, because I have been thinking about it and I just want to get it out. But I don't need any special reaction from you.

He is wide eyed. His mouth open wide shark jaw

Okay

I don't expect anything

That's okay

She closes her eyes for a prolonged second. He touches his palms with his fingertips.

You remember at the end

I do

You remember at the end?

Yes

Some of the things we did, you know, how you were different, at the end —

He's breathing quickly Yes. Yes

Her breathing is quick

She opens her mouth like shark jaws her lips part

He holds eye contact.

I want you to know — she holds eye contact

She says his name aloud

She says his name aloud

She takes a breath —

I want you to know that they weren't consensual.

Fuck
He covers his face.

He speaks through his fingers —
She leans back.

He says — In the kitchen

She fixes her eyes on him and then exhales. Yes.
She looks at him.
Then she says — But it was that whole time that
— Winter.

She moves, as if to touch her phone in her pocket.
He reaches towards her in a panic and in a panic he says —

I loved you so much

The Sound of the Sea

THE FIRST TIME that she had gone on her own, she was fifteen.

She would leave on the Thursday night. For two days she made herself meals and woke herself up in the morning and Jade and Elena came over and they pretended to be grown ups and went to bed later than they should have.

On the last night she stayed up really late. She didn't invite anyone over. All alone in the house that was big and dark warm and high ceilings quiet, she packed her suitcase.

She stood in her room. She stood in her underwear. She played music that moved down the stairs into all of the rooms of the house.

She looked at the black tree garden and the night lit street below.

The next day she left for the airport in the almost dark. She had everything that needed to be printed printed out and folded (boarding pass, boarding pass) plus all the other things (passports, phone, charger, adapter, wallet) in her handbag front inside pocket and was wearing dark grey jeans and a jumper, her little roller suitcase handle in her hand.

She locked the back door and before she left she went and rechecked and unlocked and relocked the back door. She turned the water and the heating off. She stood in the corridor. She looked at the too small adultperson in the mirror. She put on her shoes.

As she walked down the street to the high street and the tube station, she thought, this is the last cold air for the rest of the year.

She jug jugged up the Northern Line in the opposite direction to the commuter traffic to Stockwell, then Green Park which has that long interchange and then down the Piccadilly Line, the carriage slowly filling with suitcases until the tube ran above ground. They were in the suburbs. This was where they filmed *Bend It Like Beckham*. She could hear the sounds of the planes taking off.

She got to the airport tube station with three hours to go. She had timed it all perfectly and everything had come on time.

Alone in the airport fifteen years old she did the sensible thing and immediately checked in her bag. Standing alone in the wide airport lobby, she smoothed down her shirt and she found H in the big yellow A — K letters. She held her passport and her boarding pass in the queue of people wearing winter clothes and coats and pushing trolleys with big cases. At the counter she did minimal speaking. Yes. Thank you. São Paulo. Via Madrid. Thanks.

Her small light suitcase came in at 7 kilograms. Twenty kilograms was far too much. That was a lot of shampoo and conditioner and presents to be packing. A woman called Miranda with the necktie and little hat taptap typed and spoke to her in English. Yes. Thank you. São Paulo. Via Madrid. Thanks.

At security she put the toiletries that she had with her in the plastic bag. Lip balm and mini toothpaste only. They didn't search her because they never searched her. She waited in the queue. She took her shoes off and on. She passed through quickly.

On the other side, she stood under the big screen.

She packed in the same way every year. It was what she had always done since she had been old enough to use her pocket money to buy herself things. Even as a six-year-old she had felt the indignity of sharing a case with her dad. All her stuff in his bag jumbled in his case with his underpants and his stupid overcolourful swimming shorts. When he had said, *okay okay* you can have your own case and pack it yourself, if you're sure you won't forget anything, she had relieved said yes please straight away.

She packed in the same way every year. But that year there was quiet and just her and no rush rush travel chaos in the house. She had stood small in her room and begun.

Unlike her parents, she was an excellent packer. She arranged everything on the floor in front of her. She took the things she needed out of their drawers. Earlier that evening she had gone to Boots. She made four piles on the floor and put her case, which was small, on the bed.

Toiletries

Clothes (beach, unbeach, sleeping, warm, unwarm, shoes)

Books and school things

Hand luggage stuff (documents, books, phone, phone charger, wallet)

Her case was very small. She put music on.

She put the toiletries in a plastic bag and tied a knot. Before she did this she checked all the lids were screwed tight. She put the plastic bag in the inner pocket of the suitcase. Moisturiser (face), moisturiser (body), face wash, mascara and tweezers. Everything else she could buy at the pharmacy by the beach or at the airport or use somebody else's. Shampoo e condicionador. Protetor solar. Repelente.

She counted out the pairs of pants and rolled them up. She rolled up the white bikini and the one with flowers on. Bikinis with the padded bits made her feel embarrassed like a child. She put her running shoes and her yellow havaianas into the case. She held up a blue and orange and pink dress. She looked at the drawer of clothes that were too bright and stretchy. These were the clothes she got for Christmas that she could only wear in Brazil. She packed beach dresses that, with nice sandals, became dresses for the city.

She rolled them up and put them in the case. She squished the pants around them. There was no chucking in or unused corners. Everything was rolled or stuffed or pressed.

She looked at herself. She took a white dress for New Year's Eve from the hanger.

She put the books flat on top to press down the layers of clothes as tight as possible.

She separated a cold weather outfit and left it on the bed. She would wear this tomorrow and on the plane. She chose jeans and an unwoolly jumper that would fold easily to fit in her bag over the next two weeks (a jumper can be voluminous and never mind a coat), and in the outer pocket of her suitcase she left a hot weather outfit that she would change into at the airport in São Paulo.

She thought, In the morning I must remember to put my toothbrush in my hand luggage.

After she packed she waxed. Strip strip strip. Everything in order.

The airport alone for the first time was exciting.

There was a promise on the other side of security. Everyone there was waiting to go somewhere. All the rows and rows of shops. She could move light and unencumbered. It was so brightly lit you couldn't see the solstice winter outside. Her handbag was light and everything inside it was in the right pockets. There was always a bookshop and shelves and shelves of perfume and lipstick and lipliner and smelly creams and sunglasses and Christmas music was playing (*last Christmas I gave you my heart*)

She stood under the big screen. It asked her to Please Wait. She thought about the debit card in her wallet and all the stretching spare pre-flight time she had. She could sit in a restaurant and at a table and eat a meal. She could go into any of the shops and buy one small thing.

She held her bag tight to her body. She looked around herself. If she sat in a restaurant she could sit on her own at a table and order a starter, and then a main. She could even do it on the stopover in Spain although it would probably be too late at night.

The airport alone was exciting. The screen would still say Please Wait for another fifty minutes at least.

She walked to the make up section in duty free. She touched the fancy lipsticks. She took the lid off a tester and looked at it. Were you allowed to put them directly on your mouth? Was that gross?

She twisted the lipstick up and down.

Can I help you?

The shop assistant looked over at her.

She shook her head. No. No. Thanks.

She waited.

The shop assistant went back to the till.

She looked back at the shop assistant. She smeared a line of the lipstick on the back of her hand like she'd seen her vovó do in the mall. She took the lid off a slightly darker one and smeared another line on her hand. She had owned her own lipsticks before but never one of these expensive ones that came in another box outside of their plastic box. She thought about Jade and which lipstick Jade would buy.

She took the twenty pound note her dad had given her in case of a terrible emergency and spent it on a greasy cuboid of lipstick paint the colour of bright red.

She went back to the big screen and looked up at it.

There would be two flights and this was the first flight. To Madrid. Sometimes they went via Lisboa. It was much cheaper to go via somewhere like this, although it was still not cheap.

She went into the bookshop. She spent eight pounds of her own on a book that she had already read.

At the beach this year maybe she would talk to one of the boys on the beach, one of the ones who surfed or went there in the evenings. How old were they? Her age? Older? Maybe a mixture. Or she could go to the beach in the afternoon without her mum or her aunty and buy a little latinha of beer from the stall that cut open coconuts for coconut water and drink it alone with her feet in the sand and then go back to the house.

I can do that, she thought.

I can do that.

(never have I never have I ever ever ever)

When they called her gate she moved through the cold spaces that became more and more metal holding her bag, and inside it her new book and her lipstick. She sat at the end of the big terminal box. The plane wasn't boarding yet.

On the walk to the gate she had passed a British Airways flight direct, not to São Paulo but to Rio de Janeiro, nearly finished boarding. Última Chamada. She imagined a British Airways direct flight would be very nice. All the seats and curtains and safety information chequered red and blue. This was the flight that gringo bank robbers, their blonde girlfriends wearing sunglasses, got at the end of films.

She could tell from the colour of their skin and eyes and hair and height that the people getting that flight were all going for one-off two- or three-week holidays, they would be trying to see as many new different bits as possible because they'd always wanted to see Brazil – but it is such a big country, Foz Iguaçu, Jesus on the mount, maybe even a boat trip down the Amazon, Christmas at a hotel can you imagine

What they did was the opposite. The three of them went re-went to the same place with the same people and did the same things every year. And the things that changed they changed in the gaps between the Christmases – more white hair, less hair, a new boyfriend, a lost job, more chairs on the beach, a new hotel traffic traffic traffic

They were boarding. She opened her book and closed it. She texted Jade and Elena. She texted her mum.

She sat in the little plane and it moved across the concrete.

But this was only the first flight, she didn't bother getting comfortable on the first flight. Just put her bag under her chair, avoided all eye contact and got her book out. What would even happen if she didn't turn her phone off? She kept her shoes on. She didn't try to sleep. This was only the first flight. It didn't matter if she was stuck by the window and there were never any little screens.

But already on the first plane there was a shifting. People she had seen wearing big fleeces and speaking English at the check-in desk were speaking Spanish and Portuguese. Some people had way too much stuff. The plane began to move away from the airport building. On this two, three-hour journey what could really go wrong; there were many smaller European airports around whose runways could be vacated for emergency landings. The noise began. They took off. Whoosh.

The layover in Madrid was quick — only an hour and a half. She had been right — they were an hour ahead so it was already nighttime and the shops and restaurants were closed. She walked through Madrid airport past the closed shops and security. She knew it very well by now. She moved through it and through it more quickly on her own. She did not, even for one tiny second, consider walking out of the building and not getting on the next plane.

She went to the gate at the end of the big glass terminal but they weren't boarding.

People gathered by her gate and the opposite gate. Between them there was a little glass smoking booth like she'd only ever seen in Europe. She could go into the smoky smoking booth. All the shops were shut. But someone in there would give her a cigarette. She felt nervous. She had thirty minutes. Outside the airport building glass was totally dark.

She opened the booth door. Two young men inside looked at her. They both had slicked back blonde hair. They smiled at her. Oh. She made a face like she was lost and had made a mistake and closed the door. She walked back to the seats by the gate and sat back down. They wouldn't get on her flight. Her fingertips were moving. They didn't look like they would be getting on her flight. All her clothes would have smelt like smoke for the rest of the journey what had she been thinking.

She sat at the end of the big glass terminal at the end of the night and waited until the end of the queue. All the families moved around her.

Where is my bag?

Where is my boarding pass?

Where is my child?

Where is the toilet?

Cadê você

To avoid standing in the long queue she boarded last and for a moment she was the last person sitting on the seats at the end of the long and tall glass building which was tall as a house.

In the square metal tunnel, which was cold, there was another queue. She let the air steward point out her seat in Spanish as if she didn't already know what the number letter meant.

When she boarded the second plane, she felt a real shifting. These were the people making her journey. Some of them she had seen wearing fleeces speaking English at the check-in desk in London but now they were speaking Portuguese, beginning to take off their cold cold weather clothes. Looking around as she found her seat the people in the plane had less height, had darker hair and browner eyes. There were more babies and more people with way too much stuff. A whole family sitting in the wrong row.

She didn't understand how so much hand luggage was allowed. So much stuff that was weird shapes. People were jiggling babies on their lap and passing bags across the rows and the kids called out for mamãe, papai. Little children making the cramped seats look big. We're going to see Vovó!

She found her seat and sat in it, her compact bag under her compact chair. She was sitting next to a woman in the middle section by the aisle. She put her book in the little flap. The man behind her held a baby out to the woman next to her. She looked at them. She motioned to the man that they should swap seats.

Thank you.

Smile.

Thank you.

Imagina.

Brigado.

She looked across the aisle out of the porthole window. The tiny wheels pulled them from the terminal. The plane was still.

She listened for the sound.

This was the flight. This was the flight. On this flight, the long long long haul flight, as the plane pushed off from the airport terminal in Madrid in the night, she took her shoes off and tucked them under the seat in front of her. She put the big soft socks on. She took her book and her toothbrush and her phone out of her bag and put them into the little pocket. She turned her phone off. She unwrapped the blanket and wrapped it around her body and while the lights were still on and the plane paused at the top of the runway she did her seat belt and tucked the blanket in under her thighs and under her feet.

The noise began.

After wide airport lobbies, rows of shops along concourses, gated spaces around gates, the huge letters A – F, long glass walls the height of houses, slow tired late early hour queues and the seating areas around the gates, the coldness in the tunnel, the stupid little buses, the sucking puckered mouth of the plane, the rickety movable staircases, the durrrr durrrr durrrr of the engine, the last of the cold English air

The noise began.

And then, in the dark after the meal when all the people in the plane were quiet, only then she felt the great loneliness open up, some distance beneath her the distance beneath her, the great grey flat of the sea below her, which moved wide and with no visible waves.

Here was the wide mouth, the big open bellied loneliness of the Atlantic.

Of course, there had been no first trip. No stepping off the plane into the soil.

Always hot-looking São Paulo appeared under the plane. Always bright with turquoise swimming pool ovals and rectangles between every other building and even on the roofs. Where the earth was broken here it was orange. She would wait for the first discernible human to appear. And then the airport carpark, the airport buildings, the runway.

And then the clapping.

As a person who listened for each humm hrrr sound change of the plane machinery she appreciated the clapping, which was by no means undiscriminating. Because there *were* good landings — excellent landings, in fact — and there were bad landings, terrible bum bumpy watch out when opening the overhead compartments landings. And then there were difficult landings executed well — for example during a storm with high winds and noisy rain — which left everyone grateful and full of awe.

There were landings so good that you woke up already parallel to the trunks of the trees, little plane wheels whizzing like car tyres on the ground.

Going through security she could pick her passport. Pick her language. She waited for people to react with surprise but they never did.

Of course, there had been no first trip.

And then there was arriving back. *Back* back. Over the sea over the island shore. The moving back down, down down of the plane, over the sea over the island shore, over the winter bone bare fields that were usually brown and grey-brown but one year had been all white.

And then her favourite bit. And it only happened some years, on the years when there were no clouds and when the plane was made to wait its turn on the runway and when she was awake and sitting on the right side of the plane. On these years the halves of the city sprung and held apart like two hands clapped together. Beneath her known buildings rose, oriented by the curving river bone of her glass gristle city.

These years she rush rush rushed to find the house before the plane twisted and she was facing the sky again. She worked backwards outwards from the river bank — there was Big Ben, the wheel, that park was Battersea of course yes there was the power station, so that was Clapham Common or was that Wandsworth, so that railway line went to Balham, and that was her common, that square was the blue square of the Lido, which meant her house was just down one of those roads —

Stepping off the plane everything was muted. This was how it always was. This route through the airport had none of the Christmas rush of going, no red tinsel, no music and no baubles.

When she was a child, before her mother got her British citizenship, they had always had to wait for her by passport control. She stood in the other queue that moved more slowly and had more people in it. They waited until finally she approached the booth. They could half hear the questions, then half hear her sentences. She was asked what she was doing. Where was she going.

And at first she answered yes and no yes — tired but polite — yes and no and of course.

Until, not reacting like they should have to the words *I am a doctor, yes I am a doctor* she became more tired and more righteous *that is my husband and that is my daughter and this is my address*. And angry and tired and almost making a scene in yesterday's clothes, and by this point it had been weeks since she had spoken for that long in English, she said — Yes yes ok. Thank you. But after they stamped her passport and let her cross the line, she turned and said quietly, shaking *Excuse me what's your name? What is your name? Okay. Yes. I will be making a complaint. Tomorrow I will make a complaint.*

They waited for their bags in this silence.

Every year they walked to the car through the unhumid cold, the unhumid wind the unhumid grey. The quiet air had no smell and made your cheek skin chap. Everything horrid and too cold but also never quite as cold as she had thought it would be.

They drove through West London and then across the river until her places began to appear — her bus routes, her parks, her house.

The weird staid neatness of the house. Its unlit uncolours. Can't get to sleep.

Everything muted.

When she was a child —

They took the night flight leaving on the day before the last day of school, meaning that year after year she missed all its seasonal English permissiveness — the Christmas assembly where Mr. Williams sang both the girl and the boy parts from Summer Lovin', her very own nativity play, the end of term game of spin the bottle at Toby C's house which meant that Jade first kissed a boy a whole three months before her.

They piled into the car (did you lock the back door, who has the key, okay one last passport check) with unclosed prepacked suitcases waiting for the traffic to thin through Wandsworth and Fulham and on that bit of motorway before Heathrow. Her dad, who was always sure that this year would be the year they missed their expensive flights, became more nervous like — Shit shit where did all this traffic come from? What time is it? What time is it? Bugger.

In the airport he arranged their passports on the counter and their overweight bags on the scales.

No no this is my passport and this is hers and these are hers.

Do we have seats together?

Darling would you like to sit with dad or me?

What do you mean can you sit by yourself?

In the waiting space after security even through the dark, her dad looked for a seat by the glass walls. When she was little she had sat on his lap. As a very special treat on his tenth birthday, her dad had been taken by his parents to Leeds airport to watch planes take off. Even now even through the dark he liked to watch the little golden lights.

Look at that one. That's a big machine, my word. A 747 perhaps.

But as soon as she was old enough to read she had stopped.

Where do you think it's going? California? The Middle East?

Her mum would sit opposite them, not responding or participating. She unpacked and repacked her hand luggage, found and refound her boarding pass, and counted the presents and counted their corresponding relatives.

Shit shit shit.

What is it?

Oh shit

What is it

Did you buy something for Priscila's new boyfriend?

Shit.

Can you go to duty free and pick a bottle please.

Yes. Yes.

And then a look over her shoulder and in whispers –

Baby can you run to the bookshop while your dad is in duty free and buy him a book you think he'd like?

Er

The present I got him this year is very small. I've been busy!

Her mum put a note in her hand.

Don't tell him. Go. Go!

Her mother was not afraid they would miss their plane; she was terrified of falling out of the sky.

Please Wait. Go to Gate. Boarding. Last Call. Última Chamada.

But you were a great baby. Never cried. Never cried even at take off. You were a great baby. Always happy.

The first time that she had flown alone there had been some discussion, a negotiation.

Mum wouldn't you and Dad like to go early and have some time just you two, like you used to when I was younger?
Mum, I can go myself.
I'll be fifteen then, very grown up.
Can't I stay for the last day of school?
No no of course I still want to see Vovó and Vovô.
But I talk to Ana Paula on Facebook whenever I like.

Yes of course I understand how to get a flight.
I know you can't take liquids.
Mum –
I'm okay in the house alone I promise.
But *fine* if you insist I will invite Jade and Elena over.

Her parents left on the Monday night.
Byebye kiss kiss hug.
We will text you as soon as we land, you must answer the phone.
Big big hug. Abraço.
Oh you are so grown up look at you.
You know I didn't get on a plane by myself until I was twenty-seven.
Abraço

There was always here and there was always there.

Home is where the
Home is where the
Home is where

maracujá
manga
cajú

apples even

abacaxí

amora
ameixa
namora

amoras were they blackberries or mulberries or

amora
namora
enamour

what even is a gooseberry?

Only when she was older did she realise all that time
some of these fruits had been living double named double lives
one soft and wet and café da manhã

the other shrivel sour and in Sainsbury's

There was always here
and there was always

As an adult —

Adamant not to abjectly fear flying like her mother, she made elaborate plans.

In the case of a fire she would lie on the ground and feel her way out, using the poltronas. She counted how far she was from the exit before sitting down. Some planes promised emergency lights but who knew if these would turn on. She was very good at holding her breath and could put the pillow cover over her mouth. But what if the emergency door didn't open?

In the case of a collision with another plane — this one posed a serious problem. It was not covered in the safety talks or videos. The other plane might be hidden in clouds and would move at such a speed that no one would see it not even the pilot. In this case — there was no solution to this one.

In the case of a water landing, she would survive. There is no question of this. She would have her lifejacket and she would sit on something that could float like a flat part of the wing or a door. If it was a hot part of the sea even better. Even if there were sharks she would sit on the floating part of the plane or on the inflatable slide. The only problem would be those waves the size of a block of flats that come in the middle of the sea.

In the case of a hijacking — this one would also be tricky. But people liked Latin America these days (didn't they?) so on balance it seemed unlikely to happen.

In the case of a malfunction — this one she worried about. What if the crew didn't notice? It could easily happen — hubristic pilot who, affected by some external pressure either personal or professional, ignored the fatal warning signs.

In the case of someone opening a door — this one terrified her. Why would they create doors that could be opened? Was it actually possible to open the doors? If not why did they have a sign warning people not to open the door? Would they run out of oxygen? Would they all fly straight out? No she would not. She would fold her body around her armrest and she would stay there.

Of course there had been no first trip.

Only —

These huge airports
their grey, like the sea
the wideness before the sea

She held her documents, flew over the ocean

there was always here
there was always here

PART III

2015

Tiago

THE YEAR BEGAN with a bicycle.

Her parents were away, so she threw a party in the big house in Tooting. She put white lilac and silver discounted Christmas tinsel all over the kitchen and the downstairs corridor and used it to cordon off the upstairs. She hung white baubles from the banisters and door knobs. She made caipirinhas using limes and ice and sugar, and put it out in jugs ready to serve in white plastic cups when people arrived and even though it wasn't a big party Elena brought her speakers (because otherwise it wouldn't really be a party, would it?)

You must all wear white. I've told everyone coming that they must wear white.

Before it started the three of them sat together in the kitchen. They had pushed the dining table to the wall, leaving the room wide and empty and too well lit — they would turn down the lights when everyone arrived — Jade and Elena were sitting on chairs facing the middle of the room and she handed them white plastic cups. Music was playing.

Jade held the drink to her face — Fuck!

They looked at her.

Jade laughed — This reminds me of that time — except I don't think you put limes in it that time — this taste reminds me of that time in year eleven when you came back with that bottle of kuh chacha, kuh . . . how do you say it?

Cachaça! Ka-*sha*-sa!

Kuh-shaa-ser?

The doorbell rang.

It's easy to remember – she said, standing up to answer the door and leaving the room – it's easy to remember because the Cs get softer as you move through the word –

The journalist guys she worked with were at the front door. They had arrived way too early with their girlfriends, who were all called Sophie and wearing glitter on their eyelids, and their roommates, who were called Barney and wearing blazers and holding bottles of ale for the fridge, or red wine that was actually a little cold, don't open it yet – gosh I've never been this far south of the river!

Tooting is quite nice isn't it?

You never told me your house was so *large!*

Later later, just in time for the virada, some of their old friends from school, and Jade's friends from art school and their friends and their partners arrived loud and laughing, already drunk and holding open bottles of sparkling wine or vodka and lemonade mixed in the big plastic two-litre bottles, because this was what they did when they were all together again.

They spread themselves through the kitchen and down the steps under the winter-stripped rose bush into the garden. The night was dry and crisp and although their breath froze in front of them no one was cold and everyone was talking because as each person had arrived she'd put a plastic cup of caipirinha in their hand.

She stood by the kitchen door and looked around her.

Two people were dancing by the stove. Nathan who sat next to her at work had cornered Elena by the steps and Jade was standing inside interrupting the friend of the guy that Gee had brought with her. There were lights between her mother's vases and her paintings on the wall. Two of Elena's friends were dancing under the kitchen tinsel. She stood by the door by the concrete steps under the rose bush branches.

But why did you ask us all to wear white? Elena had said.

Because –

shhh

Ten!

Because –

sh

Nine!

Eight

Seven
Six

Five
Four
Three

Two

ONE

Happy

Happy happy new feliz

Feliz ano

Feliz dois mil e HAPPYNEWYEAR

And at the end of the night when they had all left at the end of the first day of the new ano novo she saw that someone had left a bicycle.

She had a good job at a big name organisation. It wasn't permanent but each time her contract ended another had come and then another. One time it was plastic surgery, the next time playboys with yachts and this time kidnappings. It turned out 2015 was going to be another important year for Latin America's biggest democracy! So she had stayed in London for Christmas because of work while her parents had gone to Brazil. It was so expensive there was no point going for just a few days anyway.

In mid late December, in the moments before her parents had left, they stood in the corridor by the front door with their two suitcases.

But will you be warm enough?

Yes.

But – should I show you how to change the settings on the boiler again?

No.

And do you have enough cash for dog food?

Yes.

Her mum pouted.

Her mum said – You know I didn't want to go without you but Vovô is getting old and –

No no obviously, of course Mum.

Okay. Her mum hugged her and almost tearing up, her mum said – Okay then baby.

Okay.

Vovô will be very impressed that your job is so important.

Yes.

Okay then

Okay
Bye
Byebye
Bye
I love you
Bye.

She closed the door.

Later, at night in the big and empty house she ran herself a hot bath with bubbles and put music on.

She got in the bath. She lit two big candles and then turned the lights off. She left the door open. There was no reason for her to get dressed or make herself meals or turn the lights on. She felt her hands turn soft.

She had planned to spend hours in this bath. But everywhere was so dark. The whole house was quiet for her.

She moved her body in the water.

She got out and lay in her bed.

She worked up until the 23rd. On Christmas Eve she woke up late in the dark morning in her dark room at the top of the big and empty house. She lay there with her eyes closed for the whole of the morning until she became hungry. Then she put on socks and turned on the landing light. She fed the dog. She made breakfast food at lunchtime and ate it on the sofa.

For her parents it would still only be the morning. They'd arranged to call her in the afternoon after they got back from the beach and after they'd all had lunch.

She lay on the sofa.

She waited on the sofa with the dog all day through the end of their night and their morning and then their afternoon, until it was time for them to call. Outside was dark.

They had arranged to call her before they did the presents. When they eventually rang, they passed her round on an ipad.

She spoke to them, headless, wearing her dressing gown. Vovô, vovó, Ana Paula, Marcos, mumãe, papai, all bright, bright colours blue orange green yellow amarelo green around them.

Feliz Natal!

Feliz Natal

Feliz Natal querida!

Is it cold there?

Sim! Yes very.

It's very sunny here very hot!

Looks lovely.

Que saudade

Feliz Natal prima!

We were at the praia this morning

I'm very jealous.
Brrr que frio que frio
But I have the heating on and the dog is here
Que linda!
We were on the beach today, I saw turtles –
Oh really how big were they?
Feliz Natal!
Que saudade
Just like this big
Everyone misses you
Quer falar com a prima –
Everyone is so interested
Abraços!
We all miss you
Grande abraço!
Feliz Natal!
Beijo
Beijo!
Tchau
Tchau tchau
Tchau querida.

In total it had lasted under fifteen minutes.

After the call ended, before deciding to turn the television on, she lay back on the sofa in the dark. Outside was very quiet. She was wearing big indoor socks wet from the bathroom floor.

She was back at work on the second day of the new year. Outside was very cold.

Her boss was a man called Gareth who was married to a famous newsreader, not that anyone mentioned that of course. The organisation was so big name it had its own cafeteria.

This was where she first saw Tiago.

The first few times that she had gone down to the basement cafeteria in the new year, he had been there with another man and she had heard them from the other side of the salad bar. She hung back holding up the queue with her tray to be sure because she could only hear a word here, a word there –

Me da aí

Puxa

Espera

Claro

And when he spoke in English she heard the accent that she would recognise anywhere, except in her mother's voice. Her face bled red when she looked at him.

The year began with a bicycle.

By the end of the week her parents were back. She was glad. She looked up their flight arrival time on her laptop and counted down from landing to disembarking to passport control to baggage claim to airport carpark to drive home, so she knew in advance when they would get to the house. When they arrived she had the table set and a little dinner hot.

Ohh! Her mother said between big hugs. But this is very nice!

No — she looked at the dinner all set out — I mean, whatever.

The next morning was a Friday. She climbed on top of the bike in the hallway before leaving for work. Put her foot on the pedal.

Her dad, his hair newly grey against his red tan face, said — You're not riding that to work are you?

And then her mum — The traffic is so dangerous!

They looked at her. They stood together on the stairs. They were both jet lagged, both in pyjamas.

She looked at them, her foot still on the pedal.

The bike was perfect, blue and just a little tall for her.

No, no. I think perhaps just around South London.

Well let me get you lights you mustn't go out without lights.

She nodded.

Yeah. Thanks.

And a shiny jacket and a helmet.

Yeah.

She got down off the bike.

She looked back at her parents and moved towards the door. She held her gloved hand up, waved, closed the front door.

Walking to the tube station she felt very cold although she had covered herself in a hat and scarf and gloves and grey woolly tights.

As soon as she stepped into the building she had been thinking about lunch. Populating a spreadsheet, her feet under her chair, she thought about lunch. At 12:20 she got up from her desk.

She got in the lift.

In the cafeteria, she says —

Obrigada

in response to a plate load of broccoli.

He says —

Opa.

Serving hand mid air, he says —

Brasileira?

Sou.

He looks around, gives her another spoonful of broccoli, winks.

Later that day walking from her office, behind her at the top of the stairs at the crushing intersection into Oxford Circus tube station, a group of white teenagers in braces and ponytails are talking about the Abercrombie store.

What are you going to buy in the Abercrombie store?
I am going to buy some of those too.
In red
Or orange
Or both?
I wish but the pound is so strong right now.

She hovers at the traffic lights, smooths down her coat, waiting for them to ask her for directions.

She goes back to the cafeteria the next day and the next. Sometimes he isn't there and she hover scans the room, holding her tray out and inevitably getting in the way of someone very busy.

From across the room he looks like he is a little taller than her, the same height if she's wearing boots. He has black hair, brown eyes, his skin is darker than her skin. He wears a white uniform.

Some days she sees him and he doesn't see her. When this happens her hands sweat around the tray plastic and she tells herself to wave *go say it*

Olá

Oi

Oi Tiago, tudo bem?

And all that first month, in the still so cold evenings she takes long baths while her parents watch the news. She uses the gel that smells like eucalyptus. She squeezes the gloopy green bubble juice into the dry tub and then she turns the taps on full, pushing the water crash into the gel against the bath tub metal creating a big thick foam.

Sometimes she turns the shower on too. But she leaves the light on. It is like being in the hot green centre of the earth.

She touches her thighs, her calves, the curve of the back of her feet

She watches her finger skin soften wrinkle ridge

This body —

The next month, like always, it rained a lot. On the way to work and on the way back from work her shoes filled with the grainy grey wet of the pavement.

One lunchtime she couldn't go to the cafeteria. Or even go to the paper bag chain lunch shops for a tub of plain rice.

The lady who cleaned the toilets had seen her nice navy blue shoe poking sideways out from under the cubicle door. (Those toilets were embarrassing at the best of times, right by the lifts in the centre of the open plan office.)

Excuse me, was she okay? Knock knock knock.

Yes! Sorry! Yesyes. Thank you. Desperate not to have to leave the cubicle and look the lady in the face, she repeated — I'm fine, aha ye-es, thanks so much, I'm fine, sorry, thank you, totally fine, just a stomach ache, ache in my stomach, I'm actually so fine. And pausing then to listen for the sounds of the woman leaving — Thanks though. Definitely starting to feel better. I feel fine. Thanks so much for checking. Thank you I'll move my foot. Sorry.

Apart from that time she was in the cafeteria every day. She thinks to herself — because outside was so cold! And buying lunch in the cafeteria was undeniably cheaper. She eats a lot of boiled vegetables.

She eats a lot of boiled vegetables but he is always on his feet and their conversations are short —

But you are brasileira?

But you grew up here?

But where were you born?

But you are English?

He greets her in Portuguese, calls her inglesinha, sometimes brasileira.

That weekend she tried out the bike. It was a little tall for her but it was fast and light and blue. Her dad had got her all the safety accessories and she screwed the lights onto the back and handle bars.

She cycled to Jade's house in Streatham. She cycled through the park, which was still bare and unleafy but beginning to squelch wet with mud and little football boots. That weekend she went to Jade's house in Streatham and they watched a film on her mini projector.

When she opened the door Jade's mum, slow smiling Jade's mum, asked her how she was. She said – I'm good. I'm great. She sat in the living room under a blanket in the warm. Jade's mum made them chicken kievs. Jade's mum said how good it was to see her. Yes.

When she left she said – Thank you for having me. And it's good to be here, to see you too.

She smiled and Jade's mum hugged her.

Later she turned her new bike lights on. She cycled back home through the common, which was something her dad would have preferred her not to do.

The next week on a Tuesday, she hangs back in the cafeteria when he is there, and after practising in her head over and over she asks – Tiago, where in Brazil do you come from?

Belo Horizonte. Have you ever been there?

Yes! Ages ago.

As she says this she remembers that when they went there it had just been to change planes, and she hadn't even left the airport.

On the next Tuesday she sees him and he sees her and he asks her how she is.

Um

What is it you do?

I erm

She bleeds all over her face

I do like reports on Brazil

I'm very busy.

She nods her head.

You know work is – she widens her eyes and, sighing like she'd seen the older adult women in the office do, she shakes her face, hands open palms on either side of her head – work is just *crazy.*

He looks at her.

Immediately, she feels embarrassed.

Ah é?

He looks at her. She touches at the sleeves of her blazer.

That evening she still felt embarrassing in the bath. Cringing she told herself to forget about it. She could never go to the cafeteria again of course. But who cares she could bring lunch in instead. Who cares

She breathes in the hot bath smell

When the bubbles die she looks down into the green-like water. She touches her belly. She touches her foot, her toes her toe nails

this foot
this foot
these feet

this leg calf and thigh thigh and

this belly
this back
these arms, hands and elbows

She still had long days when she thought

look at this broken body
look at this broken up body

On the first bright day of the year she was walking to a meeting in a new part of London when a small round woman with grey hair approached her, beginning a question in English and ending it in Portuguese.

I can help you, senhora.

She needed to find this building, she said, getting out her phone and opening a WhatsApp conversation, it was not easy to find this building.

What's the address?

She looked at the WhatsApp message.

The lady didn't have an English sim, otherwise she would have found it herself. She knew how to use Mapas, ahem.

The woman held onto her arm. She was staying with her daughter in Kilburn who had told her to come there at one p.m. to sign up for the English lessons.

I know this place. It's really close. Let me walk you over.

Her daughter was a nurse at the hospital in Hammersmith. Her husband was English, he was called Carl, and he was a software engineer. Carl was a very tall man.

Mmhmm.

In the building there was a small queue. The woman didn't let go of her arm, so they stood close to each other, together.

In the queue the lady turned to her —

And what about her? How old was she

Where was she from?

South London

No no but in Brazil where was she from?

Oh um

Then the receptionist said — Yes next please hello there.

But there had been a two-hour window!

Right

And why had she arrived right at the end of the window?

Well

She looked at the printout.

These lessons were very popular, didn't she know?

Yes yup.

Without translating she shrugged on the old woman's behalf.

The receptionist said — Can you bring your mother back tomorrow?

Um

Really, she should have come earlier.

Right

The old woman looked up.

But

You should know our English lessons are very popular.

The old woman looked at her.

She paused.

Then, putting on her most polite and reasonable and most middle-class voice, she said — Yes of course I am so sorry.

The receptionist rolled her eyes.

But — she leant forwards — but since my mother *is* already here, could she not sign up?

The receptionist rolled her eyes.

Thank you.

She smiled at the receptionist. Thank you.

I can allow your mother to sign up although I cannot *guarantee* her a place.

Smiling. Oh thank you. I really appreciate it.

She really should have come earlier.

Yes. Of course.

After hearing her explanation, the old lady frowned. But this was the time that her daughter had told her to come by? Why was it all booked up? Was it really all booked up? What else was she meant to have done? Why do they say they have a window if what they really mean is get here at eleven a.m.?

She opened her mouth to reply. There was a queue forming behind them. The meeting she was meant to be in had started.

Still too embarrassed to go back to the cafeteria, she started cooking in the evening and bringing lunch in. That week she ate it sitting at her desk but on Wednesday Nathan, who sat next to her, bought sushi and they sat eating together on the square sofas without arm rests.

As usually happened Nathan talked a lot and she listened.

I learnt Spanish in Colombia – Nathan looked at her – I worked at a mountain bike rental shop in the holidays during uni.

Oh. Nice.

I spent over four months there.

Oh did you do a year abroad?

No no I mean ahem four months cumulatively. Over two years

She frowned at him.

I don't think that's how that works, Nathan.

No yeah sorry.

She paused.

Otherwise I'd have spent like *years* of my life in –

Yeah yeah of course. Obviously.

She looked at him and then looked at her food.

I love South America. I'd love to go to Brazil

He looked at her.

Yeah? I mean you should then.

Yeah?

Yeah. The weather is pretty great.

He looked at her, listening.

She looked at her food. I mean it depends where you go I suppose obviously it's a huge country the temperature and climate vary so much

Right.

Nathan put a piece of sushi in his mouth.

Then he said – I've heard the parties are great.

Yeah –

She thought of her grandparents eating breakfast, coffee and toasted bread with cheese, and of her grandmother peeling mango for her in the morning.

Yeah.

But I'm going to America at Easter.

Where?

East coast. New York, Boston.

She took a last bite of her spaghetti and closed her tupperware.

You know Nathan, *America* is a continent, two continents in fact.

Oh

You should call it the US. Or the United States.

Oh right.

She held her tupperware in her lap.

Just FYI.

On Thursday when she had to go to the basement she avoided the big glass doors to the cafeteria. She worried that she would see Tiago in the lift or on the street by the entrance, but she didn't.

On Monday evening she stood on the tube at rush hour on the way home and on the seat closest to her a woman with long braids in a bun sat with her son, who looked about three and was wearing a red puffer jacket. And he was eating a muffin and his mum was wiping his face, and he was getting crumbs everywhere and inside his coat and she was laughing while trying to catch them.

Meu filho you are making a mess!

The kid didn't respond. He looked up and made eye contact with the woman standing above him, holding onto the ceiling rail.

She smiled at him.

He stopped eating and looked at her without smiling.

His mother followed his gaze — Sorry!

No no — Head shake, shake smile.

Tá vendo? The woman said, wiping her son's mouth again — Para com isso, no more mess! People are looking at you!

He was smiling, pouting and his mum began to laugh and as she wiped his jacket, his mum picked him up and put him in her lap and kissed him on the face.

This is what the woman standing up wants to say — Que fofinho! Que lindinho!

She tests Portuguese lines in her head with different emphasis.

Que fofo! Que lindinho!

She wants to say — You don't need to switch into English to speak to me. I'm not like the other people on this tube.

She tests Portuguese lines in her head.

The driver announces Vauxhall, and the woman does up her son's jacket and asks him if he has everything. She stands and her son stands too. She smiles.

The doors open.

As the spring began again, in the mornings which were so much brighter and lighter earlier, she began to get the trouble in the mornings again.

She sat on the toilet in a blouse and pants holding her phone, typing an email that at first said:

Hi, I'm so sorry — tube delays!

And then said:

Heya, so sorry — dog emergency!

But eventually became:

Gareth, I'm so sorry — awful cramps! In at lunch.

She didn't get dressed. She lay over the duvet on the bed in her blazer, her legs and arms and body flat.

She read the message again and pressed send. She was pleased with the last version. It was more convincing than the previous drafts, would almost certainly preclude any further enquiries from Gareth and was impossible to cross-reference with the TFL website.

But, she thought as she lay on her back, but most days it was better. Overall, it was getting better — this year the urgent need to shit only occasionally forced her out of bed in the morning. For this she was grateful.

That year she had only spent one afternoon all curled on the cold floor of the big organisation toilets. She hadn't forgotten the lady who always nodded at her with concern when they met in the loo, or by the little kitchen. She was almost sure the lady was Latin American. The lady was short like her mum but in a uniform. But she was always too whole body embarrassed to ever begin a conversation so she didn't know which country the lady was from or anything else. What would they talk about anyway Hello, hi hi yes absolutely fine ha ha thanks thank you

Still. This week she would avoid tight-waisted skirts. Undo her button after lunch. No melted cheese.

Lying on the bed, she closed her eyes. She touched her fingers on her fingers.

And as the spring began they wanted to take her out. In Peckham. Jade and Elena and this girl Gee from Jade's art school.

Hm

At least it's not Dalston, they said.

Hmm.

You don't have to drink, Jade said. You can cycle home if you want.

Fine. Okay. Fine.

So she got dressed at home. She put her make up on. She got the tube and then the Overground. She stood on the outdoors platform, her hands in her pockets.

Walking down the stairs at Peckham Rye station all together they ran into the little brother of a girl who they'd known at school.

Elena whispered his name and pointed at him.

Is that –

The other two looked at the back of the man's head, then back at Elena.

Errr

Jade leant to the side.

Yup! It is.

Jade ran ahead, stopping beside him and tapping him on his high up shoulder.

Oh my god – Jonathan?

Hey hi oh wow

Jonathan!

Jade

How are you doing? How are you?

Good great

The guy nodded at her.

Jade held her hands to the side incredulously. You're fucking massive!

Jonathan laughed.

I remember you screaming that time the tree fell down in front of the science block, you must have been in year seven you were so scared. Do you remember that?

Yes

To be fair it was a big tree

How old are you anyway?

Seventeen

Jade looked very seriously at him — What you doing out so late then?

Jonathan looked at her and then to the side.

Pause

Jade laughed — I'm joking, I'm fucking joking Jonathan!

He laughed.

They laughed.

Inside, under the moving indoor lights, three drinks down, loud heart beating, she began a conversation —

Look everyone I have a question. Okay stop listen *but I have a question.*

Ok ok —

Go!

It's a very important question. I've been thinking about it for a while and I'm baffled.

Okay shoot

They were sitting in the bar in the corner where it was quieter and you could talk.

She began —

Right so, you guys have casual sex, one night stands sometimes, yes?

Jade said — Yes I have had a couple.

Gee said — Yep yes ahem.

Elena said — Mmm. Not really.

Okay well this is a question about one night stands. Elena maybe you will still have some insights anyway.

Right.

Okay, that's fine.

The three of them looked at her.

So?

So —

Deep shallow breath — So so when you have a one night stand, you've usually been drinking the night before. Correct?

Usually

Yes most times

Not like super drunk but just happy drunk.

Yep

Well, and I think this is normal but I'm not sure —

What?

What is it?

Just say it!

Well I think this is normal but when I drink usually in the mornings I get weird . . .

Weird?

Weird belly.

Oh

Ah ha ha ha

That's normal right?

That's normal!

I get that

I always get that

It's absolutely normal

So I was wondering

Yes

When you have a one night stand, and if you like don't want to run home in the middle of the night, or like if you fall asleep, and if you've been drinking the night before, and you're there in the morning and you have a weird belly and you need to do . . . what do you do?

Jade was laughing. Elena was laughing and shaking her head. Oh my god.

Gee held her hands up — Okay okay this has happened to me! I have a technique! But firstly, yes very sensible question.

She laughed. Okay. What I do is when I go to the bathroom, and I turn all the taps on in the sink and I get the shampoo and I pour it into the sink and then make it all bubbly and shampooey fruity and I splash the steam around and . . .

Jade shook her head. But some flats have those separate toilet rooms. Where the sink is in the bathroom. Jade shook her head. I think you just have to go for it. You just have to go for it.

Elena — I would invite them out for breakfast and then do it in the cafe toilet.

She got home to the house in Tooting a little drunk quite late but not very late and lay on the sofa with her laptop open and found the seventy-nine "Tiago Miguel Da Silva"s in London. She scroll scroll scrolled.

Twelve are old-looking, and a couple have no photos just soft-coloured backgrounds with the message –

Jesus ama você <3

and

Deus é FIEL

There is a photograph of a darkened figure a man standing with the light behind him in front of the sun by the Houses of Parliament.

He's wearing a fitted denim jacket and black shorts and bad sunglasses.

She fell asleep on the sofa.

She wakes, suddenly

And how is it that everyone who did approach her for directions was Brazilian? They asked her for directions to places that she had never been like Buckingham Palace and Madame Tussauds and Harrods or the London Dungeon. Sometimes she didn't even wait for them to finish their slow English questions before replying –

Yes this is the *Victoria Line*, you need to change at *Green Park*

The museum is in that direction, there's a subway that goes to the entrance

I'm sorry I don't know where the Abercrombie store is, but this *is* Regent Street

Sometimes they started visibly when this green-grey eyed not pale white-skinned woman, whose loose fitting camel-coloured coat and black big heel boots told them she was nowhere more at home than in the stern mute lines of the European silhouette, announced herself with a floating São Paulo accent.

And nothing gratified her more than being asked – But when did you move to London?

Some of their contracts were nearly up.

So the other young people from her office wanted to drag her out to South East London.

Nathan said – You've got to come, who knows when we'll be working together again!

Let's go out *properly*, it'll be nice. Not just to the pub after work but out at the weekend.

There is a bar club place in Peckham with taxidermy, you will really like.

Okay, yes. No no of course I'll miss you. Of course!

She arrived by bike, sweaty and wet faced from the rain. Before meeting the others, she paused under a newsagent awning and put on her lipstick.

They were all sitting in a corner of the bar, which was down a set of steps.

Nathan waved at her and she walked over.

This place used to be a church didn't you know?

Oh really. She put her stuff under the table but didn't sit. She looked around at the new fake old stained glass and cocktails and palm trees drawn onto blackboards.

I can actually get a caipirinha here. And coconut water.

Hi I'll have a coconut water.

She leant forward on the bar – Can I ask, is it fresh? Thank you.

She sat down next to Nathan. She drank the coconut water and then she drank a too sweet too expensive pineapple coconut drink with rum in it. Nathan was telling a story

The people there were so lovely really

Just so welcoming, right

Absolutely absolutely

I'm still in touch with them you know, the couple who ran the place

Oh really

Really

She sank into the dark leather chairs. Tom and another guy were speaking next to her —

But did you see it coming?

No I didn't see it coming I was so hopeful right until they announced it

That was a chilling moment

I don't think anyone saw that coming

Well —

There was a real shock in the room actually when the numbers came in

By the way can I just say your lipstick is so striking

What?

Really. Your lipstick. Yes.

Oh

Would you like another drink?

Um

I'll get it no no really sit down

Oh

After one or two or possibly three hours she turned to Nathan.

You know Nathan, when I was growing up people didn't come to Peckham.

Yeah?

Well I mean obviously the people who lived here lived here

Yeah

Right

Nathan nodded. What was it like then?

I don't know. I never came here did I

She laughed.

The other guy called Sam said – So what you doing now, are you staying?

Yeah, I have –

That's great!

Yes. It's with Melanie, well she's got a lot of things on later this year. People keep being kidnapped, so

Ah ha.

Nice one.

It's lucky that you speak all those languages

Right.

Yes.

Anyway. It doesn't start for a week

So you have a sort of holiday?

Sort of yeah. I have a sort of holiday.

Are you going anywhere? Back home?

Er

She looked at him.

I'm staying in London.

I'm actually from London, I'm from South London, sort of around here but not really

Oh really?

Yes

Whereabouts

Tooting

Oh is that –

It's near Streatham, Clapham, or you might know Balham?

Right.

Yep

And you still live there?

Yes with my parents.

Oh and how is that?

It's fine. We get along.

I suppose there is a housing crisis

Yes. But also I mean it's not so awful

No I mean my flat's covered in mould and I pay

I mean for example in Brazil people often live at home until

Until?

Until they get married or move cities or

Well we should stay in touch because I don't know when I'll next –

She looked around the bar.

She turned to Nathan who sat next to her at work – God Nathan you know you know Nathan when I was growing up no one went out in Peckham

He looked at her and clapped her jovially on the shoulder.

He said her name.

Yeah yeah we know, London's changing. We know.

When she cycled home on her blue bike it was dark but she had lights.

She cycled past cemeteries down deserted high streets with small shuttered shop fronts and overfull rubbish bins, through the wide and willow curved back streets of Dulwich through

crescent

crescent crescent

grove

avenue

hill

estate

road estate

Herne Hill

which was silent until the very last moment before it became Brixton.

And through Brixton she moved past the tall town houses with ambitious growing palm trees and feather duster pampas and stained glass entrances in the quiet residential spaces between Streatham and Clapham before the dark and yellow-coloured common.

As she rode she became too hot under her clothes. There was no wind in the street light dark. She stopped in the middle of an empty residential street where no one was walking and all the cars were parked and she removed the layer layers, peeling off her tights and stuffing them in her pocket, until she reached the damp sweat-swelled hair on the small of her back and at the top of her thighs and under her belly button.

These are the same streets they used to walk down endlessly when they were sixteen looking for a park or house party to get drunk in or high in or make out with a stranger in.

Late at night in this last week in the bath she thinks about thinking about Tiago.

But –

She touches her hands on her ankles in the dark wet of the bath

But —

She wakes from a dream.

It was the first hot evening and they were eating outside on the table in the garden at ten p.m. under the huge white and yellow rose bush that her dad had planted nearly twenty years ago.

Standing, her dad said — Well thank you that was *delicious*

Good!

And now I'm going to watch the news.

And, taking his plate, he climbed the concrete steps into the kitchen.

Her mother leant back and sighed, closing her eyes. She looked at her mum. Before her mum could begin a new topic, ask her about her work or the dog or had she watched that new crime series with the man from that film they had seen together last year, she said —

Mum

Yeah?

Mum did I tell you about the Brazilian man at my work?

What Brazilian man?

The one I told you about, he works in the cafeteria.

Oh. How old is he?

I don't know. Under thirty. Maybe twenty-six.

How long has he been living here?

I don't know. A year? Two years?

What does he do at your work?

He works in the cafeteria. That's where I met him

He said he wants to study.

What does he want to study?

I don't know.

Her mother lowered her glasses.

What?

So is he good-looking?

Um I don't know.

What do you mean you don't know!

Mum

Is he handsome, like good-looking fit, "buff" do you still say "buff" — she moved her hands around

OK. If you are asking whether he conforms to traditional male beauty norms prescribed by —

Baby, why don't you invite him round?

No.

Why not?! I always invite Brazilians I know who've just arrived round I think it's nice

No no no

There's Marcia and her husband, they're coming on Thursday

No. No no

Why not?

It would be so awkward. I don't know him at all, and neither do you I mean it's not like he just arrived here, he has plenty of friends. Also I haven't seen him in ages.

Okay

Okay.

It's just an idea

Thanks for your idea

She looked away but her mother was still looking at her.

You know in my day Brazilian men were . . .

Mum I'm not going out with him.

Okay.

Pause.

In your day Brazilian men were . . .

I don't know

So why did you say it?

Well — she put her fork down — well you know I had a lot of boyfriends before your dad

Yeah

And then I moved to England.

Yeah

And then I had some more boyfriends.

Okay

Well and me and my friends — my Brazilian friends in England — we used to think the Brazilian men we knew could be difficult, more traditional.

But lots of English men are traditional.

Oh yes. That is very true. I once asked your Grandpa Simon to peel a potato and he became very distressed.

Okay so what is your point

I don't know boneca just be aware of that.

Okay. Thumbs up. Noted.

On Friday she has trouble in the morning.

Sitting on the loo in her underwear she thinks about what she'll wear. It's not cold outside. This is climate change for sure, she thinks. Spring summer never used to be like this.

She thinks about wearing the clothes she only wears in Brazil. The stretchier more colourful dresses and soft shorts that she gets for Christmas and wears in the days after over her bikini at the beach and then packs and unpacks away in the bottom drawer when she gets home.

She picks out an orange vest. It's silky and actually she bought it in London but she wears it with blue jeans and white havaianas. She takes off the havaianas and puts on shoes. She thinks about Tiago. His body in this teeming moving city, his routes her routes, her roads his roads, her bus his bus. Tiago in the cafeteria.

Okay.

Inside the card swipe building before she goes back to the basement she takes a deep breath.

The cafeteria is emptier because people are starting to eat outside. He's there, Tiago behind the counter. She holds her tray.

The pause after he serves her is longer than before.

Hi

Tudo bem?

Tudo tudo.

Okay

She smiles at him.

Brigada

She sits down. Looks at the vegetables.

He stops to leave a salt shaker on the table where she is sitting. She pauses then he says —

Where in London do you live?

I live in South London, like Clapham and Streatham around there

I also live in South London with some other brasileiros who work in the kitchen, it's a place called Tooting —

What! But —

He looks at her.

But I live in Tooting, I grew up in Tooting!

She looks up at him. She's smiling.

He puts his palms on the table top.

Vamos go for a drink sometime — he says, saying "go for a drink" in English.

(Panic —
Does he go out to the same places you go to?
Why have you never seen him on the way to work?
Does he ride a bike into work
Does he want to have a drink one on one or are his friends coming
What if it is cold or raining
Does he have English friends
Should you give him your number?
Should you ask for his number
What would you text him?
What language
What if he uses slang you don't know
What does he smell like
What does his body look like
Does he have sex with women
Does he have a girlfriend?
Who is he having sex with?
Is he going to try and fuck you
Does he want to fuck you
Do you want to fuck him?)

He says — Now the weather in this country is not so intolerable, we should have some beers on the common.

That Saturday was the first day of the year above twenty degrees. She woke up early and straight away. All the pasty English women were on the common in bikinis and all the men were playing football with their shirts off. If her tia were there she'd be wearing a fleece.

During the day she lay on the grass alone. She took her blue bike and she took a book.

She spread out her limbs and closed her eyes. Lay in a star shape.

She checked her phone. Nathan had texted her asking if she wanted to go to a Peruvian restaurant in Hackney? And also, he's just finished *Love in the Time of Cholera,* which of course she must have read, and he'd love to know what she thought?

At home that week she cooked every evening. She used YouTube videos to make beans better than her mum. She sat at the kitchen table and flicked watching the end of each of the videos and she found the beans that looked most gooey and browny red and right, and then she went to the very beginning and followed the instructions. She started with onions, garlic and bacon. Slice slicing. She put her mum's old records on and opened the kitchen door to the garden. Pressure cooker whistle cooking.

And after taking his first bite her dad smiled at her over the table.

Her mum said — This is great thank you darling.

Every time as soon as she started chopping her mum said — Can I help?

She laughed, every time saying — No Mum. Please do not help.

Look at these warm nights! Jade said.

And Elena said — Let's go out out out, you're on holiday!

You can go out without tights and the sun stays up until midnight!

No it doesn't — she said — Ten p.m. latest. We're not in Norway you know

Oh really?!

Mmhm.

But the nights were getting shorter. Not yet warm but warmer.

She wore a thin coat that was black but satin and shining like pyjamas. At the start of the night when they ran down steps and escalators to catch trains and buses her thin and open-buttoned coat flew out behind her, rising in the wind

And on the way home —

Behind her on the full and steamed up N155 at four in the very early morning in the dark hours before sunrise, she could see the outline of brown curly hair reflected in the window. Around Elephant and Castle she heard the sound of a woman's voice laughing laughing and repeating the name — Marcela Marcela

Marcela

For some reason that she can't explain –

Standing at the back of a really very nice party in Camberwell with a bunch of Jade's friends from art school who were putting on a sort of exhibition, she starts to talk about him.

She's at the back of what had been a kitchen on her phone. The back door is open and outside the sky is pink coloured.

It's just a little place, an old terraced house that's about to be turned into flats that's been stripped down, turned into a kind of gallery with fairy lights and a makeshift bar and bits of art coming out of the unplastered ceiling full of people in wide leg trousers and beards wandering around.

A girl who she's met a few times approaches her. They stand together at the back of the party. She holds out a packet of rolling tobacco.

Oh

I'm smoking, do you want one?

No, no thank you.

The girl looks at her – You alright?

Yeah yeah course

Boy trouble?

No. No

The girl is looking at her. Do you have a boyfriend?

She looks up.

No. No.

Haven't had one in years actually.

The girl smiles at her.

Yeah fuck boyfriends right

Right.

Pause.

They step outside into the garden, which is concrete, full of broken furniture and small climbing plants. The girl lights her cigarette and looks at her. Behind them the sky is watery pink

Then –

I did used to have a boyfriend

Yeah?

Yeah

It was about five years ago

Yeah

But it started seven, six years ago, when I was sixteen, fifteen.

Oh yeah? Was he your age or

Yeah a little older but not much

Always the way.

Well the boys our age were –

Yeah the worst.

Mmn.

So what happened did he disappear

No no he's still like – she moves her hands around – about.

Do you still see him?

Um

She looks out into the garden and then the sky.

He's a doctor now actually.

Fancy!

Yeah.

So what happened, did he move or?

No he stayed. He trained at the hospital near where we grew up near my house. Where my parents work.

Oh. But it didn't work out?

No

The girl looks at her. She looks into the garden and then the sky.

No it didn't work out

She looks into the garden and then the dark pink sky.

He was my first boyfriend actually. My first – everything.

She takes a long bath that night. And after and before she looks in the mirror.

She had always thought she'd have grown into a grown up body by now — bigger breasted and tall.

Yet here she was.

(never have I ever have I ever)

She looks at his name on the screen.

Lastly

You dress with the anxiety
trimming your pubes
moisturising your skin with the expensive moisturiser that smells like ripe mango

scrubbing your dolphin body in the shower bath
putting on black pants and a black bra
And the anxiety fills you with the sense of the unsexy alienness of other people's bodies, their jelly fleshy weirdness

(What does he do in Tooting?
Does he ride a bike into work
Can he afford a travelcard
Does he go out to the same places you go to?
Does his body look how you think his body looks
Who is he having sex with?
Are the people he fucks English or Brazilian?
Men and/or women?
Where does he meet people? Online? In bars?
Or on trains and in shops and on the street?
Would you fuck him if you saw him on the street?
Would you fuck him?)

Mum-mãe

ONE EVENING —

You help your mum load the dishwasher. Dad, who cooked, watches the ten o'clock news in another room.

She turns on the machine and you wipe the table. She pauses for a moment before feeding the dog.

Who wants tea?

Me.

OK.

She fills the kettle, and then as the kettle boils she feeds the dog. This is what happens after dinner.

The dishwasher and the kettle vroom wurr slush and the dog crunch crunches his food.

The water boils and she pours it on the tea bags then carries the mugs over. One mug has four black and white portrait photos of dogs looking into the camera arranged in a square with the caption "The Beagles" on it. The other says "Science Museum."

She puts the milk on the table, and then sits down. Outside is dark. She smiles and closes her eyes.

Ahh.

How was your day darling?

Good.

Did you manage to speak to the — She moves her hands around.

You frown at her. Yeah.

She nods.

You hold your mugs and listen to the kitchen sound.

You look at her.

Mum.

Yeah?

Mum.

Yeah baby?

Can you teach me the swear words in Portuguese? I don't know them, and no one in our family really swears.

She closes her eyes again. Tia Ana Paula swears. Maybe not that much in front of you.

Okay. But yeah that's what I mean. I don't even know it when people are swearing.

I can try and teach you.

Ok, cool.

Not that I've sworn in Portuguese much in the last thirty years.

She picks up her mug, hovering her nose above it to test the temperature.

You wait.

There's filho da puta, which is a very serious one

Right. You wouldn't use it?

No, no —

Do people disapprove of it?

Sim, it's frowned upon by some women, feminists.

You nod.

Also merda, you know like French.

Yes.

There's porra, which is male ejaculate.

Right.

People say like — she holds up her hands — "Porra! I can't believe that happened!"

Okay!

Foda-se, vai se fuder is like go fuck yourself. It's an irregular verb.

What does it mean?

Go fuck yourself.

You nod.

Also tomar no cu, that's the same but it means take it up the ass.

Okay.

There's also caralho, like "ah caralho!"

Ok yeah. I've heard people use that one.

It's like saying "fuck!", you know.

Ok. What does it mean?

Penis. It means penis.

Cool.

Both of you sit at the table warming your hands on the tea as it cools to a drinkable temperature.

Mum —

Yeah?

What swear words did you used to use?

I used to say, I don't know — she nods and drums her fingers on the table — we said like porra. Oh also cazzo.

Cat-zo?

Yes. It also means penis.

Right.
The etymology is Italian I believe.

She drinks her tea. You drink your tea.

Cool.
She looks at you and smiles and closes her eyes.
Thanks Mum.
It's okay boneca.

Your mother never hit you.

Yes she got angry, slammed doors, cried, had called you a bitch but only sometimes. You did all those things too.
(Crazy fiery women those latin ladies, right)

You were thirteen. Wearing skinny jeans on your unskinny legs and mascara. You were taller than your mum but still much shorter than your dad. You had just gone to the theatre.

(This is a terrible story)

The three of you were on the tube. Mum sat down. She was wearing a big blue dress.

Oval

Sit on my lap
No!
Just if you want to sit –
I don't want to sit
Okay.

Stockwell.

Clapham

Your mum put her hand on your hand.
You pull away.
Mum!

Clapham

Clapham

She says — What did you think of the play?

Silence.

I liked the costumes a lot, what did you think of the main woman, baby?

Um

What did you think, baby?

Mum don't call me that.

Your mum looks away

Okay.

Your mum looks at you.

So did you like thc play?

You pursed lips speak. It was alright.

She looks away from you, as if speaking to the carriage — I love living in this city, having all the galleries and theatres and museums

Your dad nods. Mmm.

Putting little quote fingers in the air she says — When I'm here I don't feel *foreign*

But you are *foreign*

And then you also say — Coming here and stealing all our jobs

Your dad looks at you.

Your dad panics. He says – Don't say that.
It was a joke

Your dad says – Never fucking say that
What do you mean? It's a joke
He looks at your mother.

Your mum doesn't look at you.

Balham

What
You're repeating what you've heard somewhere. Don't fucking do that.
Your mum is sitting down still and crying.
People are looking.

Look just calm down don't be angry at me I haven't done anything

Apologise to your mother
But
Apologise to your mother

Jesus
Do not swear at me young lady!

That's not swearing!
Do not answer back
Oh my god!! Ohmygod!!
You feel your throat crunch.

You don't look at your mum.

Tooting

In the house you go to your room and cry.

Later, you find your mum having a bath.
   You knock. You stand by the bathroom door.

She says your name.
   She says it in the way that even your dad can't say it.

There is a silence the size of a house.

You say –
   Mum
   Mum I'm sorry.

You hear the bath water move.

She says –
   I love you
   I love you baby.

Muhhm

Mãe
Mummy
Mamãe
Mum

Mum

How can you explain your mother who is like the buttress root of a tree spreading across the red sofa in your warm grey green living room with woolly socks on and wet hair in some kind of home dying kit bonnet from which she has carefully excluded one lock of grey, her glasses on a string around her neck which curves forward as she squints into her laptop and types with two fingers?

How can you explain your mother who had had to leave the room when dad was reading out loud the scene where the Death Eaters appear at the Quidditch World Cup. It happened again and again. Books four to seven are so dark she had said it reminds me of she had said it makes me anxious —

Your father can be silly. Very handsome also but nevertheless

When we moved in together he did not tell his mother. And it was not because he was embarrassed of me — your grandma, Grandma Suzie, actually always liked me very much. And also your Grandpa Simon. That was not the problem, they would have loved to hear that your father had found a person — they were very happy and I think relieved when we told them we were getting married — but your father would have these long conversations with his mother where they would talk about the garden and quince trees and greengage vines and the apple bushes and he would ask them whether the something something had had fruit yet, and were they going to make it into jam and perhaps he should come up soon to chop down the branch of the oak of the

And eventually I said — You should tell your mother because it will make her happy. And also because it is true. So your father called her, and that time he spent only fifteen minutes talking about the garden, and then he told her. And your grandparents were happy. They said — Oh how lovely, you must both come up and visit, and they sent us the beautiful earthenware bowls with the dripping brown and green that we still have although a couple have broken.

And they said you must come to visit. So we did. We got in the car and we drove to their house, which was the first time that I had ever gone that far north before, apart from when me and Kalpana got the train to Edinburgh for the weekend, and they were extremely welcoming and lovely. They made a dinner and we went on walks — they made us sleep in a room with twin beds, which I thought was very funny — it was all very proper

We were about to leave, saying bye bye bye with all our stuff in the car, and I was feeling very welcomed — especially by your grandma who is so loving and an affectionate person — and as your father shook hands with Grandpa Simon, I gave Grandma Suzie a kiss and a hug. Um abraço. This is the way that I greet everybody. She looked a little startled, but then I hugged your grandpa and then of course as is normal your father hugged Grandma Suzie and we got into the car and drove off.

In the car back your father was very quiet.

And then he said — You know, that is the first time I have hugged my mother in fifteen years.

But before you go to your new big school let me tell you about my school.

No it won't take very long, it will not be a long story, I can tell you it while your dad finishes making food.

I went to a school run by nuns. I went to a Catholic school run by nuns who were in a convent near the house we lived in in São Paulo. We wore these heavy ugly brown skirts, and long white socks

It was a mortifying outfit to wear as a teenager and I also had my big round glasses like the Beatles —

I was never religious.

When I was a student we thought that is not really marxism. But working educating reading reprinting sometimes in secret — we used to do it in a church. Just a small church with one room or two nothing fancy or ornate, a small church with an old old priest. I don't know what the nuns would have thought. I don't know. It is complex.

People were disappeared. My friends were tortured. I didn't see my family for years. I was very young.

I don't know my darling.

When you were fourteen –

You took a book from the bookshelf in the front room an old book with heavy dark red covers from before books were bendy and had pictures on the front.

Holding that book for the first time you thought it had come from your grandmother's house in Yorkshire

Crumble fray hard back, in old red with the golden print font

NORTHANGER
ABBEY

and the horizontal golden lines on the spine

Opening it, for the first time, that first time you saw stamped on the inside first page –

06 NOV 1980

And then in a circle crest –

BIBLIOTECA
UNIVERSIDADE DE SÃO PAULO

Dr.
Dra.

Isadora

Doutora

Dr. Amado

Dra. Amado

Doctor doctor

Isa
dora

Izz
Iz

My wife

Eu sou

Isadora

Izer door ruh

Isadora is —

One day your mum comes into the kitchen at the back of the house where the door is open to the steps to the garden, and you are cooking and you are playing her records that you have never listened to together

And Elis sings –

> Não quero lhe falar, meu grande amor
> das coisas que aprendi
> nos discos

But but

But

How can you explain your mother, who like all mothers looks very sexy and slim in some old photos, with her long curling hair and her John Lennon glasses but most unexpected of all, your mother, who no one has ever told you you resemble, in those old photos where she is hands in the air mouth open speaking straight white teeth into the camera, most unexpected of all in those old photos your mother is wearing some 1980s version of your face

Because

you speak in english
(you speak to your mother in english)

But

You do not always speak in english
at work
on the street
in the plane
or at the airport

(straight white teeth)

But when you speak, move, in those moments when you speak
you hear your mother's voice

2001

Ana Paula, A Love Story

FOR WHAT FEELS like all the days —

Depending what time her shift is, Isadora leaves for the hospital at eight a.m. rushing and kissing goodbye bye baby tchau bye. Richard leaves at eight thirty a.m., also rushing to drop off the baby, who is nine years old, at school on his way to work. Tchau tia, beijo! Bye! Tchau tchau tia.

What Ana Paula does is she goes back to bed. She eats food in bowls (pasta, cheese, cereal, rice, leftovers) and looks at the English papers on the breakfast table and thinks about reading them and then she watches TV. She sits on the sofa eating more cereal and watching those English reality TV shows that specialise in mundanity. Neil and Priscilla need £300 for a holiday in Spain. She feels scared of the outside. She is deeply ashamed of this. She does not get dressed. Bridget and Roger's mother left them a teapot they believe may be of historical significance.

On the bad days when she can't face them (sweetheart where is your bookbag? Please brush your hair. Did you brush your teeth? Richard I'm late and I'm hungry can you make me some toast? Did you do them properly? Okay let me smell your breath. Okay. Where is the jam? I don't want jam. Yes jam is made of fruit but the sugar content is very high. Dad where is my bookbag? Yes I have got shoes on. Okay bye, bye, bye, tchau tchau, we're late, okay beijo tia, byebyebye) on the days when she can't face them she lies in bed holding in her morning pee until the house goes quiet.

Ana Paula will never tell anyone this, especially not Marcos, but this is the only period in her life when she doesn't brush her teeth. Ana Paula knows she should brush at least twice a day. Ana Paula believes in brushing at least twice a day, and flossing and mouthwash and visiting the dentist every six months. But she doesn't brush her teeth. What she does if she has to leave the big house is gargle mouthwash. She stands in the bathroom next to her brush and she doesn't use it. Every so often she wets it so that it looks used. Eventually the grit around her teeth stops feeling gritty and becomes soft and furry like moss. She runs her tongue along the moss. She uses toilet paper to wipe at the moss. (what the fuck am I doing)

Each day she promises herself she will turn on the PC in the study where there are read and unread emails. She estimates that by now there will be between three and eleven in her inbox.

In the afternoon when the kids' shows start coming on (*Art Attack*, that cartoon about the Viking, that other nautical show, *Captain Pugwash*, the girl with frizzy hair in the very nice orphanage) she knows she has to clean up or hide before her niece comes back from her after school club. How did it get dark outside already? She puts on a blouse and a bra so that it looks like she's been out and changed back into pyjama trousers.

There are some days when she really has been out to class and on those days she is sweating and exhausted from speaking in English with the professor and the other students and washing and finding so many layers of clothes that match each other and then the rush hour tube ride back to Tooting in her big coat and socks.

And then the baby comes bounding in in her little red riding hood coat with the big black buttons holding her little square bookbag and speaking without stopping tells her about her day, tripping all over the tenses and conjugations and breathing her baby breath on Ana Paula's face — TodayIwentswimmingAnd GabiandElliePwasthereNotEllieGshedoesn'tlikeswimming — tiavocêtahmeovindo?

At five p.m. Ana Paula, who can't cook, puts two potatoes in the microwave with some cheddar on them, a meal which the baby calls Jacket Potato.

She asks — Jacket like coat?

The baby pauses.

Yep.

This is her first dinner. (The second will be European and when Richard and Isadora come home, maybe ratatouille or sausages and mash or roast chicken and rice and salad. Richard is a good cook.) They eat it together in front of the television, maybe they watch *Sleeping Beauty* or *Snow White* or *The Lion King*. Ana Paula hopes the baby doesn't choose *The Lion King* because then there will be crying and nose wiping and hugging and no but it'll be alright and these things happen in the animal kingdom. They watch them in Portuguese because Isadora asked her to bring over the VHSs from Brazil. A *Bela Adormecida, Branca de Neve, O Rei Leão*.

When they were at home, sitting on the sofa the baby asked her questions.

The baby asked her whether she had also learnt about the Tudors and right angle triangles.

No, I did not learn about the Tudors at school.

Oh

But yes I did learn about right angle triangles. I also had to learn English.

And did you have boys in your class?

No boys. None.

Oh.

And no boy teachers.

What?

No. I went to a school that was run by nuns. Freiras.

The baby paused. Like in *The Sound of Music*?

Like in *The Sound of Music.*

Ana Paula tugged on the baby's little polo shirt with the primary school logo on it.

And we had to wear white shirts and big heavy brown tartan skirts down to our calves.

Why?

It was the rule.

Was it hot?

It was very hot. And we had white socks that came up to our knees, and they were very hot, especially in the verão.

Oof.

We used to roll up our skirts when we left the school gates and the nuns couldn't see us.

The baby looked at Ana Paula.

But it was okay, I don't think they minded.

Were they strict and scary?

No, the nuns were nice. They were very gentle. They all remembered my big sister. Even after all those years.

Ana Paula looked at her hands.

The baby looked at her.

It had been a difficult month. The weather was turning cold and dark. They had been arguing.

Ana Paula had come home from a seminar and laid on the sofa where her sister was watching the news. She said —

So there is an English boy in my seminar, and the rumour is that he's some kind of aristocrat

What do you mean?

Isadora turned down the volume.

He is a baron or something. Or the heir. I don't know these English titles.

Oh really

Ana Paula paused. He says he's a marxist.

Isadora looked back at the television. She did not want to talk politics.

Mmm. Of course.

He is bizarre, he wears old ripped jeans and dirty shoes.

Isadora smiled and shook her head.

Anyway he has ignored me so far —

Claro.

Ana Paula moved towards her sister on the sofa.

But today he came over to tell me that he has named his cat — do you know what he has named his cat?

Isadora said nothing.

Ana Paula lowered her voice.

He has named his cat *Lula*

Her sister frowned over her glasses

After —

Yes

Isadora was quiet and then she started laughing.
Ana Paula started laughing.

After school Ana Paula takes her niece to the Science Museum.

On the tube the baby reads a book and Ana Paula holds her own book. The baby tells her when it's time to switch lines and leads her through the interchanges at Stockwell and then at Victoria. The two of them hand-held move in the opposite direction to the commuters. After the barriers at South Kensington they walk down the subway. The baby likes to run along through this tunnel ahead of her aunt. And Ana Paula likes this part of the journey. She gives the baby change for buskers. There are no cars or traffic lights and the baby can just run and disappear and appear and she doesn't have to worry.

Ana Paula must admit that the museum is excellent. World class. Surely there cannot be a better one? Or if there is it must be in New York or Tokyo or one of those Scandinavian countries.

Already since Ana Paula arrived, they have spent five whole afternoons in the interactive section, where her niece plays patiently with older and younger children. Only once has she had to intervene on baby's behalf, when a belligerent older kid started pushing her around. Otherwise Ana Paula sits on a bench, holding her course book, watching the baby and listening to the sounds of the Science Museum.

On other afternoons on other days, they spend hours in the rides section where Ana Paula has ridden the space simulator many many times because it truly is the best ride so why bother with the rest. Sometimes they visit the squiggly multicoloured basement, which really the baby is too old for but sometimes she likes to go down and check. Tia, this is where I used to play when I first came to the Science Museum. And the first cafe and the second cafe where she lets the baby order cake; and the 3D cinema.

There is one part of the museum that the baby likes to visit every time. On the top floor. Not for long, perhaps two minutes. It's a cross-section of a real Boeing 747. On the top half of the egg-shaped slice are the tiny overfamiliar details like the aisle carpet and seat belt signs and the life jackets under your seats, the blue-grey economy poltronas and the window flaps. And in the underneath bottom half of the egg shape you can see the huge thick metallic below belly of the plane.

The baby does what she does every time, she stands tiny looking up at it.

Wow.

One afternoon, when she's alone with the nine-year-old, speaking Portuguese (because she's the only person the baby did not respond to in English and secretly she is tired of hearing the English words clunk out of her mouth like massive Lego bricks), she makes pasta with pesto from the Sainsbury's jar for them to eat at five p.m.

The baby asks her what she did today and she tells her that she had met a man called Marcos in her seminar.

The baby has one question.

Is Marcos your boyfriend?

Ana Paula chews a mouthful of pesto and bow-tie shaped pasta.

Yeah.

Who's Marcos?

So who's Marcos?

Mahh-coss

Can we meet him?

In this house, when Richard was present, in this big house in Tooting, which, despite Isadora's fuxicos and her statues and her big yellow paintings, was not a Brazilian house, Ana Paula and her sister had started a second life where they spoke to each other in English.

So who's Marcos!?

I've heard from a certain source that you have a namorado called Marcos?

Is it a Spanish name? Latino? Italian? Brazilian?

And Richard said — Ana Paula they sent you to London and you found a Brazilian!

Richard laughed.

At Isadora's suggestion, Ana Paula invited Marcos to the baby's tenth birthday party. They always needed more adults and anyway there'll be cake and brigadeiros and cocktail sausages and pão de queijo, which would be a treat for him.

At first she was embarrassed by the idea. But another part of her wanted to show Marcos the house — its narrow height and English stained glass — and say, this is my sister's house. Even if inside it was too messy.

Marcos said he'd love to come. But Tooting is where? It's erm at the other end of the Northern Line. It's not far really.

Marcos arrived at the same time as all the parents, got shuffled through over a pile of shoes and wrapping paper into the TV room, which they had cleared out to make room for the noisy and bulging yellow turrets of a bouncy castle. He stood in this room, slightly trapped in between the moving wall of the castle and the solid blue wall of the room, holding a small box with a bow on it. The parents, who were used to meeting miscellaneous Brazilians around the bouncy castle at birthday parties at Isadora and Richard's, waved and smiled at him — Hullo! Hello! Alright? I'm well. How are you? I'm just dropping off my son — that's him over there in the red T-shirt I hope he doesn't get it mucky. Obree gah doh!

Marcos nodded, tried not to laugh, smiled a big-eyed smile at them.

Isadora lived through her daughter's birthdays in terror of these English mothers who spoke slowly to her because she didn't say their names right (how exactly was she meant to remember who was Kate and who was Katie and which one preferred to be called Cath). She found him, holding out food on napkins — Marr-cos! Bem-vindo! Marcos! Que prazer how lovely to meet you. Richard will take your jacket. Let me find you Ana Paula.

When he saw her Marcos was smiling. He was still wearing a huge sheepskin coat and holding the small box wrapped in paper. Ana Paula kissed him twice on the cheek.

They stood together in front of the moving yellow castle.

He said — I have never been to a party with an inflatable castle!

Ana Paula smiled. It is called a bouncy castle, like a bouncy ball.

And looking at her niece on the castle, she said — Probably she is almost too old for it.

Do you think?

Yeah. It's infantile, too childish.

But she is a child still, no?

Of course.

Ana Paula watched her niece do a roly poly. Her baby fat was not dissolving but beginning to bunch differently. She sighed. She thought — this kid will never be long and lanky like her father.

She turned to him.

Did you know something?

Marcos looked at her. He put a pão de queijo into his mouth.

So last year at her party she had a bouncy castle too

Uh huh

I wasn't here but what happened was that a little boy was crashing from side to side and ran into another kid who elbowed his face and he started crying, and when he looked up Isadora saw that he had a tooth missing — just a baby tooth — but he began to cry even more because he was scared that he would not get money for it from the tooth fairy.

The *what*?

It's like called a fada do dente, she is like Papai Noël. If you lose a tooth you put it under your pillow and in the night — she leant in and he leant in and she spoke in a lowered voice — and in the night your parents will swap it for a coin.

Aha

So Isadora and Richard had to pause the whole party and evacuate the bouncy castle to find this boy's tooth.

Marcos looked at her, his face close to her face.

And did they find it?

They did.

That evening as they put all the paper hats and tissue and paper and other endless rubbish into recycling bags, Isadora put her arm around her sister and kissed her. She said –

I like Marcos.

But you barely met him

Isadora shrugged.

E daí?

Cecília Moreira Amado was not tense or anxious or sweaty as she knew other people often were after long-haul flights. She had, as she always did, gone to the little toilet as soon as she saw the grey English floor appear under the plane. She had washed her face, brushed her teeth, powdered her face, put on her lipstick, and changed her underwear, folding the used pair into a small plastic sandwich bag that she had brought especially for this purpose. Her feet didn't hurt in their kitten heels and her underarms did not sweat in the cold English air.

Ana Paula had left her mother's house because she was tired of living there. And Cecília knew this. There had been no falling outs, like there had been with Isadora, over and over and over again, twenty years before. There were unanswered emails, but perhaps that was the way with emails. Ana Paula was older than Isadora had been. Ana Paula hadn't thrown plates or told her she was a cold-hearted bitch or told her to go fucking fuck her golpista self. But Cecília Moreira Amado, whose parents were said to have come to the big city barefoot, could tell that her youngest daughter was getting tired of her. Tired of the house that they had built her. Tired that Dona Antônia had left without saying goodbye because Cecília had always been shouting at her for cooking Cecília's family recipes wrong. Tired of São Paulo. This country where nothing worked. Tired of Brazil.

It was Isadora who had said that Ana Paula should come to London. And it was Vovô Felipe who had said that Ana Paula should apply to study there. And then who knows what would happen? And even though it had all been her idea, Isadora had laughed and said — But this is the wrong time to be leaving Brazil, no?

And Ana Paula had said — Let's swap then. You go back to São Paulo and I'll live in your big house in London.

When Isadora had said on the long-distance line that Ana Paula was bringing someone for Christmas, Vovó Cecília said — *Marcos?* Is that a Brazilian name? But was Marcos a friend from São Paulo? Why didn't she know him? Was he visiting?

On the day of their parents' flight Isadora had asked, did Ana Paula want to come to the airport? And she had said — No, there will not be space in the car, if Richard is driving.

She waited in the house, showered, did not turn on the television.

That Christmas Eve, Marcos strode into the hallway, suede shoes on the Victorian tiles, his brown hands on the textured patterned wallpaper that Isadora hated, smiling. Light brown curls falling over his face. Skiing jacket because his second cousins were Italian and had told him it would be very cold. Ohhh! He cried out and beamed and held his arms wide for each of them. Large hugs between broad shoulders and his short torso waist and booming laugh. Marcos.

And then, as Vovô Felipe stepped forward to shake his hand, Vovó Cecília's eyes widened and she felt herself pressing down her own grey lightened pulled back hair with her manicured hands, and she felt all the faces from the family photos that hadn't been on display since she got married suddenly in the corridor with her.

And Isadora stood next to her mother and said — Mãe, isn't he handsome? I think he is almost as handsome as Richard.

It was an English Christmas. Not like the ones that Richard had grown up with — oh no! — and the dinner was served on the twenty-fourth like in Brazil, but it was cold wet dark outside, and they were in the misted up inside with the heating on. In the corner of the sitting room, there was a huge Christmas tree, and when the baby shook it real pine needles fell onto the carpet.

They sat at the oak dining table in Tooting to eat Richard's Christmas dinner, served on Brazilian silverware. Richard tentatively put a Bob Dylan album on. Isadora suppressed a smile. The baby sat at the bottom of the table in a blue dress and white tights.

Richard carved the turkey. It was an organic turkey from Somerset that he had ordered and prepared especially. They sat quietly at first. And then they spoke English.

Vovô Felipe began. And where did you go to university, Marcos?

Universidade Federal do Rio de Janeiro.

That is a good university.

Yes.

What did you study?

Law.

And now?

I would like to find a job at a bank.

Ana Paula looked at her parents.

Do you think it will be easy to find such a job?

No papai of course he wouldn't find it hard.

Marcos looked at Vovô Felipe. I don't know. If that doesn't work out I will go back to Brazil.

Looking around himself he said — I want to buy a property and I don't know how realistic that will be here.

Richard swallowed his turkey. Yes. Well — he looked at Isadora — we were very lucky.

Yes we were very lucky.

It just depends what happens. With me. If I can get a job then I can get a visa and then — Marcos held his palms up and nodded.

Vovô Felipe nodded.

Marcos gave them all handpicked homely presents. They opened them after dinner, sitting on the sofas under the flashing fairy light of the Christmas tree. A long white wool scarf and gold earrings for Ana Paula, smooth carved wooden cooking spoons for Richard, a shawl for Isadora and Cecília, a pen knife for Felipe and a kid's book in Portuguese for the baby, which, if Ana Paula had thought about it properly, she would have realised he must have got his parents to post over weeks ago.

Marcos, who had five sisters, was a domestic kind of guy. After the dinner he offered to wash the dishes (something that he and his family never did for themselves at home). Richard told him not to worry, no not to worry — and with a hesitant hand on his shoulder — no not to worry the dishes could be done in the morning.

Marcos talked in Portuguese to the baby. Called her — amiga, senhora, Dona Amado — and at first she scowled and frowned, then she learnt to reply — but tio that is not my *real* name.

And of course — even before the Christmas dinner, when there were no tubes or buses and it was so cold outside — Isadora and Richard let Marcos stay over in Ana Paula's bedroom, something else which would never have happened in his mother's apartment in Rio. And without question or hesitation he preferred to be in the house with them, despite his nice flat in Euston and the long length of the Northern Line.

And in the week before Christmas, in the red green festive fuzz, he had gone to the Science Museum with her and Ana Paula, and when the baby said she had something special to show him, he had said — Oba! He was so excited! And when they stood under the Boeing 747 he reached for Ana Paula's hand.

Marcos, who had five sisters, was a domestic kind of man. And so during that winter when they dressed and undressed for bed and when he went for runs on the common and when they undressed and dressed in the morning, Ana Paula would go downstairs to have breakfast with him and in that way she began to brush her teeth again. Marcos handed the floss to her like it was the most natural thing in the world.

There had been one evening.

They lay in her bed. Not for the first time in the room overlooking the garden in the big house in Tooting, in the English winter darkness that was closing locking around the autumn. Neither of them had ever seen a season do that to the tree leaves or to the length of the daylight, pushing people indoors to put on kettles and buy thick coats and walk around with wet soaking feet and their heads in umbrellas.

She hadn't known him more than six weeks. She had only been in London four months – really she was barely getting to grips with the underground zones and peak times and only knew part of one bus route –

They lay in her bed. They were both clean smelling of soap and mouthwash, him wearing light blue cotton pyjamas and her in an LSE T-shirt and shorts. Outside was dark and the window glass was misted wet. The house was warm but the bed was warmest.

He lay on his back, his eyes closed no glasses. She turned herself in the bed towards him, a hand under his ear.

She had begun by saying his name.

And he had turned his head to her, his hair crush against the pillow, his eyes about to open.

She whispered his name – Marcos

And, her hand under his ear, she had asked him – Marcos, do you have plans for Christmas?

He looked at her. Ana Paula. She was imagining that he might be alone. He closed his eyes. And in that moment, he cancelled all his own plans and flights and said, simply —

Não.

Ana Paula leant into his clean-smelling smiling body.

With him she began to re-feel how slow motion erotic the way that another person moves their mouth could be. And the way they take off their glasses and close their eyes. They slotted into and onto each other. He ran his thumb down the inside curve of her body and the skin where he kissed her was like where the rain falls on snow.

This was Marcos.

Coragem Alfredo

WE WERE MEDICAL students living in the city.

We had a lovely little apartment me and Edi and this guy called Alfredo. I must have been what nineteen or twenty

Duda had the most chaotic flat down the road in Vila Madalena, near the bridge that was this dusty pink colour. Her flatmates were proper punks, like they used to steal my tapes from my car and when I asked for them back they said no because I was studying to be a doctor and would have more income than them. Redistribute! they said.

Anyway

Edi is Edi you know Edi he lives in Salvador now. He works in psychiatry at the university. Lives with his partner Maurício.

But Alfredo. You don't know Alfredo. I lost touch with him twenty years ago. In fact I don't know what happened to Alfredo. But Alfredo had just come to live with us. He came from a little town in the interior called Tatuí where he had trained to be a priest. Yes he had trained to be a priest went to priest seminary school had robes — he showed us pictures of him wearing the big Catholic robes, a teenager really wearing the big purple priest robes — but he left. I can't remember why but anyway he left. Maybe just he didn't like it or maybe he fell in love with someone. But he left. He left and came to São Paulo which was where he met us.

So Alfredo was new to the city. I can't even remember what he was doing. It was the early eighties, everything was chaos you know the ditadura and we were all students so you know so we were fighting fighting fighting — you know, fist in the air — clean water, free press, democracy bla bla

Me and Edi and Alfredo wanted to do graffiti. Yes paint messages over the public walls — in secret at night of course because that was the only time that you could really do it, those were difficult times

So we bought the paint and we had our black night clothes and things — I used to be very fit you know, just like you, rode a bicycle, whatever — and we were all ready to go with our paint and black clothes in the middle of the night when little Alfredo said he didn't want to come anymore. He was too scared. Poor Alfredo he was new in the big city and they were very scary times, very scary times if you were caught

Anyway

So we left the flat, me and Edi, we said that's okay Alfredo bye bye Alfredo. We went out into the night. We had decided before that we would paint political slogans and then poetry also. Because we read a lot of poetry, as well as Marx and Engels and Lenin. Sometimes things are both of course.

There was a huge wall under a bridge near where we lived, it was a sort of a late night dusty pink colour. So we painted on it in huge black letters —

C O R A G E M   A L F R E D O

And it became like, what do you call it now, a meme. Lots of people saw it. Everybody saw it. It stayed there for ages, huge big black letters across the wall under the bridge. Everybody in the city saw it. And people would say to each other would say and they would whisper *coragem!*

Coragem Alfredo!

Leaving (Coming)

YOU WERE SITTING in the kitchen with Jade, Elena and Gee. You had ordered food, so when you felt your phone vibrating in your pocket you started walking to the front door but it turned out it was your mum calling to say that Vovô Felipe had died.

Your mum had just got off the phone to your tia Ana Paula. Mum had known something was wrong as soon as she saw the São Paulo number come up on the house phone. Ana Paula hated international calling rates, she hated the fuzzy line, she hated house phones. But you can't tell your sister that your dad has died via WhatsApp. She hadn't called the house phone since you were a kid.

Mum was looking up flights and crying.

For tomorrow. I found a flight for the morning. We can pay. We knew this was going to happen. Okay baby? I love you.

I love you too.

You stood alone by the front door holding your phone. Fuck.

When you walked in the kitchen door the three of them were holding plates and cutlery and setting the table. But when they saw your face they piled on top of you and you snotted into Elena's hair as you told them that your vovô had died.

You said – My mum called. We're going to Brazil tomorrow.

Elena stroked your hair.

I have to tell work.

And then Jade said – We'll help you pack.

Okay.

Yeah we'll do it together.
Let's do it now.
Okay?
Let's do it now.
Thank you.
Jade held your hand.

The four of you sat in your bedroom. You lay on the bed with your head touching Elena's knee and Jade's hand on your face and for a while no one spoke.

And then you stood up, wiped your nose and took a case from under the bed and opened it. Elena was smiling at you. You began slowly to pull things from the wardrobe and put them into piles. (Tops, shorts, pants, dresses, shoes, sandals, earrings — bikini? *Bikini?*)

Your phone rang again, and you all looked at it, but it wasn't your mum, so Gee said — I'll get it, I'll get it.

Elena went to get plates and forks and when Jade came back with all the food Gee spread it out on the bed around you.

How you feeling?

Sad. You rub your face. But also — you throw some pants into the corner of the case — but also this is what is meant to happen, you die when you're old and you've built a family and a house and a life.

Yeah absolutely.

He did what he wanted to do with his life

That's kinda great.

Yeah he has one daughter who's a lawyer and another who's a doctor in England, that's the dream right?

Jade, who was a third generation kid, confirmed – Yup that's the dream.

You knelt to roll the pants into the corner of the case.

What about your grandma?

Gee said – Would she come live with you here?

No way.

Because it's too far?

No. And it's not because of the language either. She won't go live with my aunt. She's just got things set up there. She has some people on her street she plays cards with, a lady who cooks her food, she leaves out bananas for the hummingbirds every day after breakfast.

That's nice.

Yeah it is. For her it is.

Elena looked at you.

How long were they married?

Sixty years? They got married when she was twenty-one, I think. Vovô was a bit older like twenty-four.

Jade pursed her whole face with distaste. Elena and Gee looked at her.

Jade covered her mouth with her hand – Shit.

Pause.

You started laughing – Sixty years of marriage does sound kind of fucking grim!

Jade started laughing – I'm sorry –

You laughed.

Elena's hand, which was holding a pot of moisturiser, started to shake as she laughed.

You laughed so hard.

But – Gee said – But if I had to get married now to have sex, I would.

I don't know.

Jade scrunched up her face.

Elena shook her head.

Well, I'd definitely consider it.

Even if there were no condoms?

Jade was shaking her head. Sixty years though.

Gee nodded. Yeah I reckon so. She passed you a pair of socks.

Elena spoke for the first time. Even if there were condoms I wouldn't do it.

She shook her head.

The sex would have been shit, thrust thrust thrust *ughh*

You laughed. Because now it's so different!

It can be – Gee said.

Also people did have oral sex and whatnot back then too. Jade held a pair of havaianas in the air like a question mark. What do you think lesbians were doing?

Okay, ycs obviously.

Well exactly.

Gee resumed – Okay, okay but if you wanted to have sex with a man or didn't want to do it in secret and be ostracised, then you would have to get married? And then do you think that married women were not having good sex?

I don't know. Do you think they were coming?

Jade offered – Maybe.

Elena said – Not from their husbands.

Gee said — Well my granny had three husbands, the last one when she was seventy-five.

Jade looked impressed.

Granny Penny had three husbands?

Yup.

Jade nodded her head. You know this is something I think about a lot.

Jade paused and looked at you. I think about all the couples I used to idolise.

What like your mum and Andy?

There's my mum, and my aunties, but also I think about all the couples *historically*. Like whether Darcy was going down on Elizabeth —

No!

Yes!

You gagged on your food.

But but after giving it a lot of thought I think he was because, *because* — Jade held her hands up like a teacher, asking for silence — firstly, he takes *pride* in fairness, secondly he'll go out of his way to please her, and likes to get a job done — "nothing would be done that he didn't do himself" and thirdly, the whole second half of the book is about how he learns to *follow her instructions*. Right? Like I don't know about Bingley going down on Jane. And there's all those scenes of Mr. Darcy bathing, so we know that they have access to good hygiene for the time. Colin Firth from the lake definitely was doing it anyway. That's what that whole lake scene is about you know. Diving in, navigating the underwater bush, getting wet . . .

Pause.

You are so right.

Yeah! Thank you.

You are so right.

Like I don't think anyone was going down on Daisy in *Great Gatsby.* And that was Gatsby's downfall to be honest.

True.

So true.

Although she had been quiet for a while it felt like Elena was repeating herself. She was sitting on the bed surrounded by plates and tissues. But even now it's normal for women not to come.

Not like every time.

Or like not most of the time.

Jade said — I don't climax from just penetration.

Gee looked surprised.

You said — Me neither. For me sex is cool, but *coming* is something I do alone.

Really?

Jade said — You never told me that.

But when you went out with Leo

It just didn't happen.

They looked at you. You sat on the case with clothes on your lap.

It just didn't happen.

Elena said — But you were with Leo for *ages*

You shrugged.

Like *years*

You shrugged.

You never told me about this.

Or me.

Or me.

It's fine.

You stood up to take a dress down from the wardrobe.

And after what happened — I just didn't want to for ages.

Everyone was quiet.

Don't be weird

Sorry —

Oh

And anyway there's a good ending — you looked at the clothes in your lap — I mean it's cheesy. I was googling this and there are all these recommendations for couples to try like go on holiday or wear special underwear or whatever. So I left it because I didn't have a partner. But recently I had some money from my job and living at home and whatever so I spent some time researching vibrators — because there's a lot of them and they're all quite different — and I found one that was very highly rated and I bought it and some tingly lube and I booked out a fancy hotel room in the countryside, and just went by myself.

Oh my god are you kidding. Jade sat with her mouth open.

Nope. It was amazing like purple mood lighting and silk sheets and bath salts.

Fuck off!

How much did it cost?

All together? Three hundred pounds, for the room, train tickets and the vibrators.

What!!!

Oh my god

Best three hundred pounds I ever spent.

Seriously.

Jade was lying down covering her face laughing.
  Gee was crying with laughter and shaking her head.
  The bed was shaking with laughter.

You were lying on the closed suitcase. Outside was dark. Electronics, yes. Toiletries, yes. Documents, yes. Hot weather clothes, airplane clothes, sleep clothes, yes. Beach clothes? Funeral clothes? You had to call your mum and ask what people wore at funerals in Brazil. You zipped the case up. You must remember to put your toothbrush in your hand luggage in the morning. Outside was dark. You laid on the suitcase.

The others were lying on the bed. Elena said — I still wouldn't get married for sixty years.

Would you get married at all?

Elena paused. I don't know.

There was quiet.

But you know, I wouldn't blame my mother if she left. Elena said.

What do you mean?

Like I look at my mother and I wouldn't blame her if she left my dad, or had left us ages ago.

Pause. Gee said quietly — Me neither.

You lay on the suitcase.

Jade said — When my mum left my dad, I did used to blame her. Obviously not anymore. He used to go through her phone, asking her, who's this? Who's this? Why did you text them? And other things too but

Your stepdad is good though.

Yeah. She looked at you. Andy is alright. I don't think he's anything special but he treats her with respect, and it meant we lived in a nicer house and got to go to see my cousins nearly every year. And now my mum's done her masters. She has a job she loves. It's alright. It is good.

You looked at Jade.

Elena shook her head. She said — I don't think my mum would ever leave. My dad works and actually my mum works too, but she does all the housework and all the cooking. That isn't even the bad bit. He's angry too. After my mum does all that for him my dad is still an angry man. He has this thing that he would never hit any of us because his dad used to hit him. So instead he's like *do not talk to me like that! I will not have my daughter talk to me like that!*

Gee put on a deep dad voice and knelt on the bed, waving a finger — *Who do you think you are? I will not be spoken to like that!*

He's like *I am your father, I put food on your table*! But it's like, actually Mum does that, so.

Elcna laughed.

Yes!

So true.

But they're close, they're friends, they have sex — I hear it sometimes and they're always touching each other. When it's good, it's good. Shc gavc up her life in Italy for him, you know, she was a nurse there, he was on holiday — Elena laughed again — they fell in love, she came here. Now she works in a doctor's surgery as a receptionist.

Elena shrugged.

I don't know if I would do that for someone. I don't want to.

But if I was married or had someone's baby, then how could I say no? So no, I wouldn't blame her if she left him. But I would be surprised.

Hm.

There was a pause.

Yeah. Gee was frowning. I never thought about it. My parents don't talk about their feelings to me and probably not to each other either. She laughed. Mum spends a lot of time gardening, looking after the house, she talks to her sister on the phone a lot. I don't think they have sex. My mum doesn't even like to wear clothes that show her upper arms. Or like maybe they have sex just on birthdays. Or maybe my dad has sex with other people. Gee paused. I wouldn't blame her if she left. But she won't.

They looked at you

I don't know. I don't know. You felt awkward. Actually, actually I'd be more worried about my dad.

Jade laughed at this – Poor Richard!

My mum is the centre of his life. He has his GP practice, he likes his work. But not like she loves her work. And she has all her reproductive medicine friends here and back in Brazil too and she could live anywhere, she's made it on two fucking continents you know? She would leave such an emptiness in my dad's life. He talks about her all the time, when she's travelling they talk every day.

That's sweet.

Well

That *is* sweet.

No. Yes. I don't mean to seem ungrateful

Gee cocked her head, listening. Elena and Jade were looking at you.

You sat up.

But but, what I'm saying is she would never leave him because he could never ever leave her. Who would he cook dinner for? Who would he tell things to? Like we always say that he's incapable of keeping a secret from her because of that time he told her about her surprise birthday party.

Gee said — They always look like they have a perfect marriage.

You pause.

Yeah. But also no. I don't know. When I was little they used to argue, they used to argue all the time. And she would shout and cry, say I'm leaving. I'm leaving!

Elena joined in — *I'm leaving this family!*

And Jade — *I'm leaving this family for good, and you will see how you cope without me!*

And Gee — My mum used to say that too.

Yeah

Yep.

Yeah. She said she would go back to Italy. And she would storm out and we would find her in McDonald's eating chicken nuggets.

You lay on the suitcase. Outside was dark. Gee leant back on the bed and Jade and Elena were quiet.

And there was a pause as each of you ask yourselves —

Are these the words that circle in every mother's mouth?
I will leave this family
I am leaving this family

At night you lie next to Elena and Jade in the bed.

You have never asked your mum whether she has had an abortion
    or been raped
    or abused
    or had sex with a woman
    or whether she climaxes through penetrative sex

Fit your husband around your life, don't fit your life around your husband.

Love your child and give them everything, but build a life that is your own first.

This is what your mum had told you, telepathically, all your life.

But you weren't sure you wanted a husband
    Or a child

    Or to wrap your life around another person's life

2015

Christmas

THE PLANE FLEW in, and because the landing was smooth and flat (and because outside of the windows was warm and big leafed and green), the passengers clapped.

This is what it means to wake up rolling onto the tarmac outside São Paulo three days before Christmas. Bumbum bump. When you were a child it had meant stepping off the plane into the hot wet air thick with the juicy smell of petroleum. Later it meant moving through the air-conditioned glass walkway from the plane to the terminal, the first touch smell of Brazil delayed until the big wide room divided by the passport checking booths where you could show your blue passport and respond to the officer in Portuguese like a migrant coming home for Christmas.

And after baggage claim, which was, as you remember it, always quick (apart from times when your bags never came), and after walking along the walls made from opaque glass, shoes clack clacking on the shiny stone floor, the automatic doors opened onto the concourse.

Two figures who shrink greyed every year waved at you, holding an empty trolley for you.

Querida!

Netinha!

Kiss kiss kiss kiss.

And you would cross the vast open multi-floored room past the Christmas tree which reached to the top of the escalator, and they would buy you a pão de queijo and an ice cream, even though you had thrown these up in the car on the way to the house on the beach in both 1996 and 1998.

This year, one thin figure met you, holding no trolley. She was wearing bootleg trousers and a light blue blouse, her black hair straight and neat. She was reading something on her phone until she saw you. She was almost your height. She held her arms out to you —

Querida!

kiss

Tia!

kiss

How are you?

Good!

Are you okay taking the case?

Yes, yes. How are you?

Oh you know, you know.

Good?

Good.

She smiled at you, looking at you.

You looked around the airport.

Before we get in the car, can I grab something to eat?

Yeah sure what do you want?

Just something from the padaria.

Do you have cash?

Pause.

No. Sorry!

No no don't be silly.

You joined the queue. What do you want? Pão de queijo? Suco de manga?

Oh yes actually suco and a pão de queijo.

You stood together and she ordered for you.

You were quiet and you looked around the airport room.

Ana Paula paid and handed you the food and drink.

Thank you!

No no.

Ana Paula watched you as you stood and ate.

Do you want to sit?

No (chew) no (swallow) it's ok

Ok.

You finished off the pão de queijo and stuffed the greasy paper in your pocket.

Ana Paula frowned and held her hand out. At first you pretended to be puzzled but then you handed over the wrapper.

How was the flight?

Yeah fine, you know.

You began to walk. Ana Paula put the wrapper in the bin. Did they clap when your plane landed?

Less this year actually.

Good. It's so annoying!

Yeah?

Only Brazilians. Only Brazilians.

Again you walked through automatic glass doors, into the hot summer daytime. Under your shirt sweat collected in your armpits and ran down the arm pulling the suitcase. You walked into the carpark.

Your mother and your father are already at the beach.

Oh yes, she sent me a picture.

Of them?

Of my dad. Swimming.

Yes. He swims long distances every day. He brings his goggles to the beach.

Sounds about right.

I'm parked over here — Ana Paula said, indicating a large black SUV.

Oh wow. Your car.

I know, it's too big but.

Ana Paula shrugged.

You got in the big car.

She reversed. The car moved out and onto the big road with brown red mud and big bladed grass and Marriotts and big airport hotels on either side.

Ana Paula said — You see those building works? There was meant to be a train line by now.

You looked out of the window. Oh really? To the city centre?

Yes. It was promised, you know, you know how this country is

Delays?

Delays delays, corruption.

Corruption.

I wouldn't need a car like this if I could get a train direct, but as it is . . .

Yeah. There is a bus service though, right?

Sure. But what major cities do not have rail links to their airports? I mean with the traffic the way it is.

You think? I mean yeah, sure.

But anyway. How are you? What have you been working on? Still their *insider Brazilian*?

You cringed.

Well I work in the ideas department you know it takes a while for the ideas to become programmes and often they don't even get that far and so not much has come out that I've worked on, which is not to say I haven't been working, if you know what I mean. If you know what I mean.

With Ana Paula the Portuguese words always lodge like big Lego bricks in your mouth. Uh huh.

You looked at her and she looked at the road.

I did pitch to them a story about police brutality in Brazil, you know because of all the stuff in the USA

What?

You know tia like police violence? Because of the five you know the five black boys

Well – said Ana Paula, overtaking a truck – yeah there is a lot of poverty and criminality it is a big problem in Brazil.

They didn't go for it in the end.

Oh well.

Ana Paula turned the car down a slip road off the main road, away from the city.

They, you know, they kept trying to get me onto sports or to do something sporty Brazilian you know like football or –

Or girls in bikinis playing vôlei.

Yeah, yeah! Anyway I said no, or I didn't say no but I didn't have any ideas.

Yes. Sometimes that is wisest.

Yes.

Ana Paula waited at the traffic lights.

You should pitch them something about corruption.

Yeah?

You know this government is so corrupt meu deus I mean it's so tiring, it makes you want to hide your taxes under your mattress. You know everyone is stealing money, money, money.

Yeah.

But anyway you can read about it anywhere in the Brazilian press. The international press — the English-language press — does not cover these problems like they should, they don't write about the corruption or the way that things don't work and the way that this country is moving backwards . . . And of course in Brazil most people also think like this because they are fooled you know, because they just aren't educated. There is so much ignorância — she hit the steering wheel — ignorância is ruining this country.

Pause.

I haven't seen you since before the election. The election was . . . you followed the election? It was just terrible, she is terrible, an embarrassment like a little pathetic puppet you know?

Oh right.

Presidenta

Yeah.

You know she calls herself presiden-*tah*

Yes. I did know that.

You know it's like it's not even grammatically real, she's just made up a feminised —

Yes, I know.

Pause

Yes I did know that.

I mean the polling was also so precarious before, it was showing her not doing well, I wonder, well you know everything is so corrupt I wonder

You turned to look at your aunt and, collapsing into English, said — You think the polling was *rigged?*

Well how could it have been so wrong? I just find that . . . you know I mean polling is a *science* —

Tia, you know there was a polling crisis in the UK as well this year?

But the UK is different.

You looked at her and took care not to speak too quickly — Also also the history of polling is very young in Brazil, I was reading about it in *FT*, you know, *The Financial Times* newspaper, people *some* people think that because of the success of polling in the US that polling is always very accurate, but actually the history of polling you know the backlog of data —

Ana Paula wasn't listening — Anyway most people are outraged but you don't read about it anyway in English.

The car moved past billboards and piled unsymmetrical houses.

You wanted to ask your aunt which English news sources she was reading, but instead you said — The thing is, tia, lots of governments are corrupt. There was a government corruption scandal in England only a few years ago. It's not news.

Ah. Ana Paula waved her hand before changing gear — I will never understand what is news and what isn't. That Brazilian man who was shot in Stockwell when I was living there. Why was that such an outrage? He was much more likely to have been shot if he had stayed in Rio and they wouldn't have reported on that.

You stayed silent.

You moved along the motorway through thinning houses into mountains, into the forest.

You and your parents — Richard and Isadora and baby, the three from England — had started spending Christmas in this house behind the gates only recently after Vovó Cecília's little yellow house by the beach had been sold. After that happened one of Marcos' brothers-in-law, who was the son of someone to do with sugar, had bought this house in the new condo with guards by the beach.

You and Ana Paula arrived just in time for lunch. About ten of them were around the table, which was on the veranda and looked out to the sand and the sea, eating rice and beans and farofa and fish and some leftover pieces of beef and onions. It was not a proper lunch, you know, just something that Dona Elisabete had thrown together. Leftovers. Isadora and Richard both burnt looking and beaming rose immediately to greet their only child.

You hugged Isadora, and then you hugged Richard.

And then the rest of them rose, Lucas, kiss kiss! Marcos! Tia Celina, kiss kiss! Vovózinha! Prima Sônia, que saudade! Her boyfriend João, kiss kiss! Marcos' nephew João Pedro, kiss kiss! Paulinho, you remember Paulinho? His wife, their friend who was recently divorced and had no one to stay with — Kiss, kiss hug. Hug. Kiss, kiss hug. Oi! Tudo bom? Hug hug kiss! But you've grown so much! Hug beijo beijo beijo

Marcos' family was like the huge Latin American family that people always thought you had. He had five sisters and they had husbands (apart from the one who did not have a husband) and they had children of all ages and they uploaded pictures of each other together to Facebook and ran into each other in shopping malls and had loud conversations on speakerphone with their sons or nieces who had moved to Brasília or Recife or Belo Horizonte.

One of the cousins, a small pale guy with big curly hair and glasses, resumed his seat next to Richard quickly. He was speaking slowly and seriously in English. Richard turned to his wife and daughter, and said — You remember Guilherme, José's son, and his sister Gabi.

A woman in her twenties with brown eyes smiled and said *nice to meet you* in English and unable to stop yourself you interrupt — I speak Portuguese I speak Portuguese

Gabi laughed — *Prazer.*

Guilherme cleared his throat. He was facing Richard. I was saying to you —

Yes. Richard paused. So tell me again the topic of your thesis?

Guilherme cleared his throat. It is about the military dictatorship's relationship with student movements in the seventies and eighties —

Isadora interrupted — You see Richard! How time has passed and I am history now!

Isadora put her hand on Richard's neck and squeezed her daughter's shoulders.

Oh really? Guilherme turned to face Isadora for the first time. When were you studying?

In the eighties.

And where?

At USP.

And what did you study?

Medicina

And when did you leave?

Eighty-six.

And who funded your study?

The UK and Brazilian governments — joint.

Richard raised his eyebrows. Well — Isadora, I think you will find this young man's thesis very interesting indeed.

Oh yes?

Yes.

Guilherme pushed up his glasses.

You see what the research is showing is that the dictatorship was funding a lot of foreign graduate study in that era, in order to, you know . . .

What?

To get rid of people.

There was a pause.

I don't know, perhaps you left too late, but could be.

You looked at your mother but she was laughing. She shook her head. She put her arm around her English husband.

The hot sea breeze blew across their faces.

That night the three of you lie in the three single beds in the room at the back of the house that you share. It reminds you of being a child again. You can hear Dona Elisabete's television next door and the sound of a man speaking. In the years that you've been coming here, this has been your room at the back of the yard by Dona Elisabete. And it had been the same in Vovó's little yellow house, where you had slept in the little concrete outhouse.

Eternal guests — passed around from cousin to aunty to old friend to new friend — you always ended up in these rooms. They were always hot, sometimes without windows, narrow and unpainted.

That night the room was not tidy. Full of suitcase overspill and clothes and bottles of mosquito repellent and sun cream and shampoo and drying bikini bottoms and presents that haven't been wrapped and a roll of wrapping paper and no sellotape and your mum's canga still covered in sand and your closed neat case and then your dad's goggles and his too colourful shorts.

Your dad brushes his teeth. Your mum brushes her teeth. Have you seen my reading glasses? They are on the shelf. Have you seen *my* reading glasses. They are by the sink. They prepare for bed.

Richard likes to hear the sound of the sea, but Isadora says don't be ridiculous we must close the shutters because of the mosquitoes, besides Marcos has bought us a fan.

You feel like a child again.

Boa noite darling

Boa noite

When Isadora and Richard and baby arrived from London for the first time, Vovô and Vovó had driven the three of you straight from the airport to the beach to the yellow house. We have just done up the yellow house, Vovô Felipe had said. There are white tiles now and it is freshly yellow painted and there is air conditioning, and of course I promised you a pool.

Mum and Dad and Vovó and Vovô and Ana Paula and baby and suitcases you didn't all fit in one car and Vovó Cecília had always claimed you for her car at the airport, and Vovô Felipe would say, then you must come with me on the way back or I will be heartbroken young lady, and so you would strike a deal.

Some years you had got stuck in the holiday traffic on the motorway. You had spent hours between green and orange and blue wooden trucks and rainforest mountains and waterfalls and sometimes you had driven right through clouds as well as past the interminable tunnels. When the traffic was good you used to hold your breath when you went through tunnels. It was from the trucks that you had learnt that there was a place called SALVADOR – BA, and a place called GOIANIA – GO, and RECIFE – PE.

And five years ago when you pulled into the village of Camburí at the end of the drive at the end of the journey from England, Richard had said it was a pity to lose the soft red colour of the road when they paved it over.

But Ana Paula, turning the steering wheel, had corrected him – This is much easier to drive on, Richard, the old road was full of potholes, remember?

That evening you played cards after dinner on the veranda.

Behind you past the wall, lowleaf plants crawled into the white yellow sand of the beach. Behind you, you could hear the sound of the sea, which moved in low waves, blue and white, blue and white.

This is the place where you read Harry Potters six and seven and Tracy Beaker and *Mansfield Park* and *Beloved* and *The Color Purple* and had forced yourself through *Oliver Twist* and had tried to read Camões and gave up.

Going Out

In the early nighttime, outside was hot dark blue sky and the sound of the sea.

Ana Paula had told you that Gabi and Guilherme were going to take you out to a shit bar in the next village and that you should go it would be fun. But all the clothes you have are either too black or beige or too smart casual. There's a mirror in the concrete grey bathroom. You're not in the city. You stand in your pants. You will never fit in until you bring yourself to wear denim like Brazilians wear denim. You know this.

You're wearing a denim jumpsuit and a blue shirt and — no no

You're wearing black jeans and a black silk shirt and red lipstick — no no too hot

You're wearing a woolly crop top and black jeans — yes but too hot

Earlier that day when you were lying in the sun with a book on your face you had heard a child calling your name.

She was naked, dancing moving her bum from side to side and shaking the sea water out of her hair.

Asking to be looked at, she said your name.

And you laughed and sat up and shook your hair also.

Then Marcos' apologetic sister came to collect her daughter — Isabela, Isa-be-LA, you must not dance like this — and winking — it's what the gringos expect of us — and winking — so don't do it in front of your cousin from England.

Wink.

You're wearing the jumpsuit and a lacy bra — no way

You're wearing a top Ana Paula gave you for Christmas last year.

You lean close to the mirror and run the kohl pencil against the edge of your eyelids, and it smudges soft in the light sweat heat.

You're wearing denim hot pants you made from an old pair of flared jeans you bought when you were fourteen (why did you cut them so short? How short is too short?)

Knock knock

Let's go?

Gabi is wearing a loose blue dress and silver hoop earrings. She has a beer in her hand.

You put that dangly flower earring into your right ear.

Okay.

Okay! Vamos —

She hands you a beer.

She calls across the garden — Guilherme!

The three of you get in the car, you in the back. Guilherme, who doesn't have a licence, sits in the passenger seat. He puts on a track that you don't know. You drive with the windows down along the road cut from the side of the forest coast.

With one hand on the steering wheel, Gabi says — What kind of music do you like?

Um

(You hate this question)

Guilherme interrupts, turning around — Do you like Brazilian music?

I like Caetano Veloso.

Ei! — Guilherme claps — I like Caetano. He is very good.

He shuffles around the glove compartment for a CD. The little car bow bends along the road and through the night.

The bar in the next village has a shiny wooden structure, beams across the ceiling and the floor and white plastic chairs and a TV playing a novela. In the corner, some old crinkly guys drink beer. Outside it is so blue black dark, and your body has forgotten what it feels like to be cold.

You sit on white plastic chairs by a white plastic table. Without asking, Gabi brings over two large bottles of beer in coolers and pours it out.

You clink glasses.

Guilherme touches his glasses. I have a question. Is it true that in England you drink warm beer?

You pause to compose a diplomatic answer.

English people would not say that their beer is warm — you put your hand on the beer in front of you — but it is true that in Brazil, beer is served colder.

He nods. He sighs.

Brazilian beer is not very good.

No?

No — he waves a hand and crosses his legs — it's so light, there are no small beer producers so the big companies they just produce this — he waves again — this crap.

I like Brazilian beer.

Guilherme smiles at you. Good.

Gabi asks – Have you heard the story of what happened when Nigella Lawson came to Brazil?

They were so honoured to have her that on this chat show they decided to present her with *a traditional Brazilian food.*

Do you know what it was?

Guilherme interrupts – *Mortadella.* And to their mortification, she said –

She said that *actually* Italy was quite close to England, and she frequently visits Italy and she *frequently eats mortadella.*

You look at Gabi, and then you look at Guilherme.

Guilherme shakes his head, his eyes closed. Only in Brazil.

And Gabi shakes her head too.

You talk like this for a while. Did you watch *Doctor Who*? And where were you when Amy died? And Princessa Diana? What was your view on this royal family business? As you drink, you start to feel the Portuguese words stretch soft in your mouth like melted cheese. Your accent stops catching between your teeth. You start to laugh. As the nighttime passes the bar slowly fills and you finish two bottles of beer and Guilherme buys two more – no I insist – and two more – no I insist! – and the hum hum hum of the night gets loud and Gabi and Guilherme start a game of pool and someone is smoking a spliff and people get more chairs and start dancing.

Gabi nudges Guilherme – she nods towards a tall woman with short hair standing by the bar. The tall woman is looking at Guilherme.

Guilherme looks at her. He coughs.

Gabi laughs.

He looks up at you, then he looks at Gabi and then he hands you the cue and goes to dance with the tall woman by the bar.

Gabi shrugs, she smiles at you. You remember Guilherme sitting next to Richard speaking earnestly in English, and laugh.

You take a drink of your cold beer.

You play pool with Gabi.

You don't know how to play pool.

When you go to the toilet a man stops you —

Oi

Oi

I heard you talking about London

Yes

Do you know London?

Yes

Yes! Abbey Road!

Yes! You laugh — Yes Abbey Road!

I have visited London. To see my aunt, she lives in Croydon, do you know it?

Croydon? Yes!

Yes!

There's a train that goes there from near my house.

But — the man leans forward, looking at you, his fringe over his face — but I have to say that I am more excited about going to Liverpool.

Oh really?

Yes. Oh yes. Next time I go I would like to go to Liverpool.

You know — you say, hearing your accent fill into the room like water falling off clingfilm — you know, I would also like to go to Liverpool.

And then the golden snitch — When did you move to London?

It is a hot and blue black night.

From across the room Gabi calls your name.

You open your mouth to reply, and when you speak you hear your mother's voice.

There is one generalisation that is allowed

Brazil's beaches are the most beautiful beaches in the world.
And it is true.

This beach has —
hot white sand
blue sea
hip shoulder height waves, the right height for jumping over or diving under
big irregular volcanic rocks for rock climbing on each side
occasional turtles
islands in the distance
and, if you swim far away enough from the shore, huge green sweaty mountains.

(These are the things that should not be on beaches: piers, pebbles, towels, wet suits.)

The beach is called camburí, cambury, cam-bu-ry (or as Richard would say, cahhhm-boo-ree)

And if you drive alongside the sea you find the other words that litter the coast like bones
camburí
boiçucanga
ubatuba
caraguatatuba

guarujá

ibirapuera
ipanema

pipoca
maracujá
jabuticaba
cajú
abacaxí
oi

aba — caxí

a
ba
ca
XÍ

A B A C A X Í

Camburí beach
5.30 am 23rd December 2015

This is where, at five in the morning, Gabi asks you – Is it true that you English people have to be drunk to dance?

You stand up, finishing your beer. You stand, in the loose sand only slightly tipsy. On one side of you is the path to the house and on the other side is the wet flat sand and the tongue of the sea.

You say – But there is only one way to know that.

She looks at you, you move your body, slowly. Caetano sings tinny music into the night. He says, *you don't know me at all*. You move your body.

She stands up.
She stands in front of you. She moves her body, slowly. She dances, and you laugh and your laughter fills the night. Behind you the waves crush onto the sand.

You move your body.

And then she puts her right hand on your waist and holds your right hand in her left and her eyes ask you the question.

She knows that you don't know the dance (but you do know it a bit) and inside the closeness of her right arm she moves you off the sand in a two step two step, two step two step.

You do not verbalise the movements of your body. You concentrate on letting your body follow her body. Behind you the waves crush onto the sand.

Your body moves
(her body moves)
Your body moves —

Acknowledgments

I have been very lucky. I wrote this book in all kinds of places, but primarily the public libraries: thank you to the British Library and the Whitechapel Idea Store. I wrote also in cafes, bookshops, on the Northern Line in London, by the sea on the São Paulo coast, on airplanes and sitting on airport trolleys. Throughout my life, I have been able to move freely between the two countries where my family are. For this I am grateful.

Thank you to everyone at HMH who worked on the book—Maria Mann, Hannah Harlow, Chloe Foster, Katja Jylkka, and Beth Fuller—thank you especially for your diligence and patience copyediting, proofreading, and typesetting this unconventional (and, I suppose, stubborn) text. Christopher Moisan, thank you for the sublime cover illustration. And thank you most of all to Pilar Garcia-Brown—for your incision, your insight, and *just getting it straight away*; I have been so lucky to work with you.

Thank you to my agent Imogen Pelham for believing in *Stubborn Archivist* from when I first sent it to you in spring 2016. Thank you for loving its Londonness and its silences, for nurturing and protecting them and finding it a home in the UK and US.

Thank you to everyone who read early drafts (especially Roland Walters). Thank you to the friends whose sure, loud, and unconditional belief in me made me believe, wildly, that I could write a novel: Vi Tran, Ben Cross, Shana Allen-Holder, Babatunde Williams, Naomi Credé, Janet Eastham (you have been here for the longest time), Vinay Anicatt (thank you, so infinitely), Loukia Koumi, Maeve Scullion, Charlie Goodman, Nathalie Wright (special thanks for sitting with me and talking through the text with such intellectual rigour and patience), and Atri Banerjee.

I owe more than words can say to my mum and dad, Laura Rodrigues and Chris Fowler, for giving me this hybrid name and life, and for bringing me up surrounded by love and books and politics. (Crucially also—for providing financial security and a place to live in London.) And to my brother, George Rodrigues-Fowler, for always being on my side.

Thank you to my extended big family: Cleide and Hannah da Silva, both sets of grandparents, the Rodrigues clan, os Akamine Vasconcellos (especially Lala for being exactly the age of the baby while I was redrafting), and the Fowlers (including Evans, Atwells, and Knaptons), Darcy, Thália e Ricardo and family, Maria and family, Leslie and family, Oona and Chiara, JA, Claudia and family, Agostino, and Cleo (special thanks for talking me through South London abortion clinics in the early 1990s). Thank you, Ankhi Mukherjee, Norah Harding, and the women of Latin American Women's Aid.

Thank you always, and with my whole heart, to Irene Papavassiliou.

About the Author

Yara Rodrigues Fowler grew up in a Brazilian-British household in South London, where she is still based. Her writing has appeared in *Vogue*, *Skin Deep*, *Litro*, and other publications. She was named one of the *Observer*'s "hottest-tipped" debut novelists of 2019.

Yara is a trustee of Latin American Women's Aid, an organization that runs the only two refuges in Europe for and by Latin American women.

Stubborn Archivist is her first book. Yara was granted the Society of Authors' John C. Lawrence Award toward research for her second.